Dre,
Missed you and looks
forward to seeing you soon!!
Enjoy!
Dad

BOOK THREE

a toast to Justice

By David S. Tanz

D1502141

Copyright © 2013 David S. Tanz
All rights reserved.
ISBN: 1482309092
ISBN 13: 9781482309096
Library of Congress Control Number: 2013901933
CreateSpace Independent Publishing Platform
North Charleston, South Carolina

Part 1

CHAPTER ONE

Ashley Stone gently slid the covers off being careful not to wake him. His breathing was even, his chest expanding and contracting in a predictable cadence. When her feet hit the floor, she grabbed a large beach towel hanging on the chair along with her glass of unfinished wine and approached the sliding glass door which opened to the balcony and the panoramic view.

Stepping outside, she pushed the cushiony chair toward the direction of the upcoming final sunrise of their vacation. She noticed a small mango colored semicircle emerging on the eastern horizon which now separated the black backdrop of the Caribbean into varying shades of grey and steel blue. She lit a cigarette, which she limited to three a day for times when she wanted to think and clear her mind. As the orange tip glowed in front of her, she exhaled a conical stream of smoke which appeared as clouds on the lightening background. The slight crashing of the waves became more audible as the orange rays of the sun skimmed off of the white foamy caps of saltwater.

Her thoughts turned to her partner in crime, which was a misnomer as he was actually her partner in crime solving. Stephen Davis was her boss, her friend, her teacher and, in fewer times than she cared for, her lover. The pair had been influential in solving a series of crimes that had gripped Philadelphia only weeks before this respite. Although dating in the workplace was not looked upon favorably, the two kept their relationship as low key as possible and under the radar.

But Stone loved this man: his six-foot-two-inches of well-toned muscles, his dark wavy hair and the brains to match his classic good looks. In her mind it was a complete package. The biggest obstacles in taking the next step were his lack of commitment to a relationship and his borderline obsession with his job. Whenever she had broached the subject, he was deft at diverting the discussion so as not to meet it head on. He had said that he loved her company, was sexually turned on and satisfied by her, and enjoyed her skills when they worked as a team. He promised that if she gave him some more time, he would eventually see how foolish he was being and would succumb to a more serious relationship. Single, in her mid-thirties and still curious about having children, she consented, but also stated that the countdown clock had begun and that she might not be available forever.

She took the final drag on her Marlboro Ultra and attempted a smoke ring, which looked more like a flat tire. She laughed as she extinguished the cigarette, shot down the last of the wine and headed back into the room. As she closed the sliding glass door, she was hit by a burst of cold air, compiments of the thermostat being set on 66 degrees, which immediately froze her exposed nipples. Knowing their flight didn't depart until three o'clock and he liked an early breakfast, she was less subtle with her entry back to bed.

She knelt down at the foot of the bed and spread his splayed legs with a touch of her cold fingertips. They opened wider as he began to awake from her gingerly touch. As his head lifted, he saw her mouth open as her tongue began to outline the skin below his growing erection. Hearing a slight moan of acknowledgement and pleasure, she enveloped all of him, adding a well-timed bobbing of her head. As her speed and tightness around him increased, so did the up and down motion of his hips and torso. No words were spoken as their eyes intermittently met, but that was more than sufficient. Within moments, he climaxed as they both let out harmonic groans of pleasure.

Silently, eyes still upon her, he turned her over onto her back and mimicked her recent actions, the only difference being anatomy, but yielding the same desired results. He slowly made it back to his original position before her sensual assault, both smiling broadly.

"I can't believe that it's Monday already. It feels like we just got here," Ashley said in a truly disappointed manner.

CHAPTER TWO

The temperature reading located at the bottom right hand corner of the screen during the FOX29 morning news report indicated that it was thirty-three degrees with a wind chill making it feel like twenty. The Roundhouse, Philadelphia's aptly named police building, was warm and toasty. The usual crew of the Organized Crime Task Force, which included Michael Davis, Jim Kelly, Gerald Elkland and some newer members, awaited the return of their boss, Stephen Davis and his traveling companion and team member, Ashley Stone. The term girlfriend was avoided not only because he was their boss, but also because no one knew the status of their relationship nor wanted to guess. They showed up together looking well rested, tanned and bearing gifts.

"What the hell is going on? I leave for a few days and everyone is just mulling around," Davis said jokingly.

"Busted," said his brother, Michael, and everything returned to normal as if he had never left.

Davis and Stone handed out the token gifts; Puerto Rican Rum, Jamaican coffee, some t-shirts with lame sayings, and the standard shot glasses and refrigerator magnets with scantily clad women. The crew mentioned that they had kept the city safe while Davis was away, and that the upcoming Grand Jury meeting involving the New York mob bosses was still on schedule. They were calling for a speedy trial even before any indictments were handed down, hoping the Feds would not get their witnesses and case together in time. Phones starting ringing and Davis readied himself for his return to work and the pages of e-mails that awaited him.

As he began, the Julian Gando case crept back into his consciousness. While on vacation he had done a damn good job of avoiding any thought of work and the cases that lingered. Gando was being held in protective custody, having cut a deal after being caught and threatened with serious jail time for the commission of at least three recent murders. He had admitted to those crimes only after agreeing to a sweet deal for witness protection. He went on to implicate three New York crime family heads that had paid him to do their dirty work. It was a series of tough police work and uncontrollable circumstances that led to his arrest. Offering up those higher on the food chain in return for his protection, he was now ready to work with the Federal government who had been trying to bring these guys down for what seemed like an eternity.

Gando was being shuffled around to various locations in Delaware, New Jersey and Pennsylvania, hoping to avoid the long arm of the mob and the bounty on his head. So far his protectors had been successful with not even a near miss or attempt on his life. The other fear was that one of their own would be tempted with a large sum of money to reveal his location, but that had not occurred, either. The good news was that the Grand Jury hearing was near and a court date would be set before the New Year arrived. That date couldn't come quickly enough.

CHAPTER THREE

Jaime Valle awoke as any other morning, but today would be different. She currently resided in Cherry Hill, New Jersey, one of the more desirable and fashionable places to live outside of Philadelphia. She had grown up farther south in an area populated with more farmland and fewer people. She was the only female child, having three brothers which led to her tomboy attitude and competitive nature. Her looks were anything but that of a tomboy, though. She had piercing yet inviting Cerulean blue eyes that could captivate anyone. She had just turned thirty-two but her clear and glowing complexion made her age indeterminable. She was five-foot-five and her body was as perfect as the rest of her features. She was employed both as a dental technician several days a week and as a photographer on weekends, doing weddings and corporate events. On occasion, she would freelance for local area newspapers. She had grown up with a love for the outdoors, taking pictures, hiking and even hunting, which was one way to show up her brothers; she could outshoot every one of them and it pissed them off. She still did some shooting, but mostly in local competitions, as she had lost the urge to hunt…until now.

She felt alone, not having her recently deceased husband to accompany her on the morning walk with Cosmo, the overweight, overfriendly lab mix they had found on the patio one winter morning. After countless calls to shelters and veterinary hospitals, they adopted him rather than surrender him to the local shelter. He quickly became a devoted part of the family. He even lived in harmony with their resident cat, Oscar. Being Tuesday, it was a day off, having to work only Monday, Wednesday and Thursday at her hygienist job. It would be a different kind of a work day, but one that would be a necessary evil.

* *

The city of Philadelphia is a destination city for many reasons. For one, it contains many historic landmarks and attractions which are the foundation of this country. Philadelphia's food, riverfront and diversities also attract many tourists. The Philadelphia Convention Center, which opened in 1993, has hosted many internationally attended events, such as the Flower Show, Mummers Parade finale and even political conventions. On this particular week, it would be the home to the National Insurance Convention, hosting seminars, meetings and events for the public. Since the government bailout of many companies during the economic slowdown in the late 2000's, insurance companies have pretty much recovered. Their much criticized lack of compassion for their clients has been countered with television commercials featuring down-to-earth spokespersons such as the Gecko, Flo the sixties looking diva, and the guy who makes hairballs to set aflame. On the less likeable side are the nerd who has three arms and makes art forms on walls, the psycho who hangs onto a car, and various other losers. Since consumer confidence runs quite low in the area of insurance companies, the national meeting in Philadelphia would attempt to change that impression. Today they would kick off a new campaign to win over the critics and Philadelphia was the first stop. After the morning meetings, the companies would host a free lunch event at Constitution Center, where they could launch the new image that they created.

* *

Having finished the morning walk and disposing of Cosmo's deposits, Jaime climbed the stairs to her second floor bedroom. She pulled the white sweater over her head, removed her jeans and readied for a warm shower. She dropped the last of her undergarments on the bathroom floor and entered the shower. As the water graced her skin, she mentally went over the check list for today's agenda: wig, oversized sunglasses, light coat to go over her warmer one, and gloves. Her bag was already packed with all of the necessary tools for her task. She kept telling herself it was the right thing to do, not just for her husband, but also for all those who might face a similar injustice. She was the one to make them respond and make them do the right thing.

She got in her car, which was sitting in front of her three bedroom condo, noticing how the structure's wood was aging and turning a light grey. She started the car and set the station to KYW news radio, waiting for the traffic report that was updated every ten minutes. She really had no interest in any news story, but only in what affected her immediate world. Since the untimely death of her husband, nothing was really of any consequence to her daily existence.

She turned onto Route 70 heading west towards the Ben Franklin Bridge. She removed her EZ-Pass to avoid any proof of her trip into the city. "I must be watching too many crime shows," she thought to herself, and smiled. She stopped for gas, as the prices were fairly lower in New Jersey than over the bridge, and paid in cash. She tried to be as non-descript as possible, keeping her sunglasses over her memorable eyes, even though the clouds were still obscuring any light from the sun.

After crossing the bridge, she navigated the two-lane one-way streets, parking several short blocks from the Constitution Center. Opened in 2003 and located two blocks from the Liberty Bell, it is a relative newcomer to the plethora of history Philadelphia has to offer. One of its missions is to inspire acts of citizenship, which is exactly what she had in mind.

A crowd was materializing. Checking her watch, she saw it was 11:-28, roughly half an hour before the festivities were to commence. She tightly grasped the duffel she had removed from the car and inconspicuously headed toward her destination. She casually entered a building on Market Street. The building was tall enough and had an unobstructedz view of Independence National Historical Park in front of the Constitution Center below. This was where the planned events were to take place. It was a fair distance from where the Convention Center was situated and she hoped that the schedule would be closely adhered to. And she knew the rifle had more than sufficient range to cover that distance.

Jaime found the stairway she had selected and began to climb the several stories to the roof. The elevator was not an option as she wanted to remain as invisible as possible. When she arrived at the summit, she found the door still unlocked. This was strange in the 9/11 era. Donning her gloves, she turned the doorknob and entered the tar-coated rooftop. Her watch now read 11: 48.

She found the cinderblock she had chosen, the one with a clear view of the podium. She set the duffle next to her and unzipped the bag. She removed her .308 Winchester from it, the Bushnell tactical scope already attached. Her confidence was a given, and she decided to forgo a tripod. She took deep breaths, tried not to over-think, and waited for her prey. She was recalling all that her father had taught her on her many hunting excursions: line up the sight, hold your breath and gently squeeze the trigger.

At 11:56, the first cars pulled up to the venue. First to exit were some men is business suits, laughing at who knew what. The distinctive blue uniforms of the Philadelphia Police Department were growing in number. In succession, two more cars pulled up, one being a limo. More suits.

Jaime continued to control her breathing and focus. Her mind was oblivious to her surroundings other than the task at hand. Although she had no clear target in mind, she knew that she would act when her gut feeling told her to.

At 11:59, three familiar figures emerged from the limousine. The first was a nerdy looking guy in a suit, one of the acting spokespeople for the company that claimed to "be on your side." He disgusted her. He was followed by a beehive-haired sixties-styled woman, also recognizable. Lastly, two large green limbs appeared, followed by the lizard-like head and body. Without any hesitation, she squeezed the trigger three times in succession. The nerdy guy dropped like a stone, crimson spewing from his neatly combed hair. The green costumed figure dropped next, the green and red colors associated with the holiday season taking on a whole other meaning. The woman grabbed her shoulder and also fell to the pavement, quickly covered up by two blue uniforms. Within seconds, her gun had been stashed in the duffle and the wig and sunglasses now adorned her new persona. She also double checked to make sure there was no evidence of her being there.

The crowd was now attuned to what was happening. Jaime grabbed the handle of her Nike bag and swiftly headed toward the rooftop exit and down the concrete-lined stairwell. The sound of approaching sirens grew louder as she passed a stenciled wall that indicated the second floor. She pulled her sleeve over her hand as she turned the knob on the exit door which deposited her in an empty alleyway. Her car was three blocks away. She turned onto Sixth and walked briskly to her car, noticing an increase in decibels and men in blue. Some ran by her.

She removed the key from her pocket and her hand nervously tried to insert it into the lock. It felt like hours before it finally opened. She tossed the duffel in the rear seat and started the engine. The Ben Franklin Bridge, her only focus, was four blocks away. Her rear view mirror displayed flashing red and blue lights approaching at a high rate of speed. The police cruiser passed her in the left lane and the brake lights flared as the car screeched to a skidding halt, parked diagonal to the traffic flow. The officer jumped out. As she slowed down, he yelled to her, "Ma'am, please step on the gas and clear this area, NOW!" which was not what she was expecting to hear. Paranoia runs deep. Her heartbeat slowed to where it was inaudible, and she entered the down span of the bridge.

She hadn't yet had time to contemplate the full implications of her recent actions. There would be time for that later. She pushed the on button of the radio, wanting to hear the late breaking story on KYW, the city's all-news-all-the-time station.

"In late breaking news, Center City Philadelphia came to a complete standstill at the noon hour, as three familiar television spokespeople were struck by gunfire. During an afternoon of what was to be a free lunch for the public, sponsored by various insurance companies attending a convention in the city, shots rang out. Police suspect that this was a planned attack as three shots found their marks. All three victims were rushed to nearby Thomas Jefferson Hospital, where their conditions remain guarded."

The announcer paused for a long second before continuing.

"Two of the victims were widely known for their portrayal of comical sales people for well-known insurance companies. The third was dressed in the familiar gecko outfit. Police are not yet speculating on a motive, but the person firing the shots has yet to be identified and is being called an experienced sharpshooter. Stay tuned for more news as we cover this unfolding story. In other news...."

Jaime tapped the button and the car was thrust into silence. She was almost home.

She pulled into her driveway and rested her head on the steering wheel. Her mind was racing as she shut the engine; her emotions were a mixture of guilt, satisfaction and confusion. She came out of her zone, grabbed the bag in the rear seat and exited the car. Nervously unlocking the door, she tossed the bag in the hallway and ran to the bathroom. Her nerves were racing at undulating speed and only subsided as she violently threw up. Feeling better physically, she entered the kitchen and poured a straight shot of Kettle One, the strongest sedative in the house. Two minutes and two shots later, she entered the office and sat at her desk. She needed to rationalize and accept the events she had just put into motion.

CHAPTER FOUR

The crime scene was now cordoned off. A sea of blue uniforms was canvassing the area, seeking any potential suspects as well as any observant witnesses. Yellow crime scene tape fluttered in the soft breeze that swirled around the plaza at the Constitution Center. In contrast, blaring sirens emitted ear-splitting, high pitched warnings as they raced to the scene. News trucks sprouted up like plants on steroids as the media licked their chops. Crime scene investigators were gloved up, high stepping to the area covered in red patches. Hollywood would have been proud as the scene took on an eerie, surrealistic setting.

Stephen Davis and his squad were called in due to the proximity of their office to the crime scene and the fact that there were no pressing cases of an extreme priority. Several high ranking members of the police department made their presence felt, handing out assignments to expedite the investigation. Beat cops were going door to door, seeking out witnesses who may have noticed anything or anyone out of place. Reporters were being informed as to the ongoing events, mostly being fed the "no comment at this time" statement. There were more questions than answers: who perpetrated the crime, why, where did the shots originate from, were the victims specifically targeted and what was the motive? The answers would come in time, but not soon enough to quash fears that would emerge from this seemingly senseless event.

The latest update, not released to the public, was that one victim was critical but the two others were not in life threatening situations. Davis was told to send two members of his squad to the hospital to get statements; he sent Eckland and Kelly to Jefferson Hospital. Eckland, nicknamed "Geek," was the computer guru who had been instrumental in solving several high profile cases as of late. His expertise was not limited to the computer's inner workings; he was also adept at asking it the right questions, leading to the right answers and directions.

A mobile unit parked in front of the Constitution Center was serving as the headquarters to disseminate information. Davis was one of several officers taking incoming information. Witness reports came in as well license plate numbers, all duly cataloged. After several hours, there were still no glaring leads that would produce a rapid closure to this case. Philadelphia would be thrust negatively into the national spotlight, and it would affect not only its reputation but also the dollars brought in by tourists and conventions.

****

Jaime was curled up in a ball on the couch, still trembling from the events that transpired hours ago. Feelings of guilt for the victims played most heavily on her. But she also felt a sense of righteousness for doing something that she believed we all wanted to do. We all pay premiums to these large insurance companies. What we pay for is protection and services if our health and well-being are compromised.

Several months ago, Jaime's husband, Jeffery, was diagnosed with a small defect in his heart. This defect was diagnosed as a mild cardiomy-opathy, a weakness in his heart muscle. The couple jumped through all of the hoops that the specialist and insurance company required. The specialist decided that an exploratory procedure would be the best course of action to determine the treatment necessary to correct his problem. The insurance doctors recommended that a change in diet and a regimen of prescription medicines would be more cost-effective. After several months of phone calls and diagnoses, the surgery was finally allowed to be scheduled. Jeffery was admitted to the hospital that evening, his wife, family and friends all in attendance for moral support. The next morning, the insurance company had put a hold on the procedure again while the blood work was scrutinized by another insurance physician. This physician concluded that a regimen of different medications and a specific diet might alleviate the problem. Jeffery could be a bit hot-headed; he was concerned about his health, and exploded with rage at the news of the delay in his procedure. Phone calls and arguments ensued and continued throughout the day. Unfortunately, the stress and emotional torture he had been subjected to had taken its toll and he passed away suddenly that night. Jeffery had lost the battle.

Jaime was awakened that night by a phone call from the hospital and she was informed that her husband had succumbed to a massive stroke and embolism, taking his life before he could be given the attention his heart had needed. She was devastated. But she was more outraged at the insurance provider that had caused the unnecessary and untimely death of this thirty-two year old seemingly healthy man.

She made countless calls and wrote countless letters to anyone who would listen to her story. All fell upon deaf ears with not even any words of condolence. This enraged her. She thought of numerous ways to make people aware of the injustice she had suffered. They had played by the rules. Jeffery had been going to school to prepare for a new career. He had been laid off recently from a middle management position in a restaurant chain that had closed almost half of its locations. He had lost his benefits, and, because Jaime didn't work full time, his insurance had covered them both. Thus, they now paid a substantial premium for private health care.

Jaime was a competitive woman, mainly because she grew up with three competitive siblings. When she was in high school, she didn't want to just be a cheerleader; she wanted to be the captain. In her two-year dental program, she didn't want to just graduate; she wanted to be first in her class. In both cases, she was. When Jeffery met his untimely and unnecessary death, she couldn't just let it pass or go unnoticed. She had to make a statement and let everyone know that it was both preventable as well as a moral injustice. This was the reason for her actions.

But she was far from done; her next step was to make her actions known to the American public. She wanted them to know what she had gone through in the hope that this miscarriage of justice would not be thrust upon anyone else. At the same time, she did not want to get caught. She wanted to be a martyr and crusader without the recognition that some people crave. Slowly, her fears and trepidations were willowing away, injecting her spirit with a new sense of purpose and motivation.

As she watched the early news reports of the ongoing investigation, a feeling of fulfillment pulsed through her. She had always been an over-achiever in anything she set out to accomplish. She did things right and to the best of her abilities, which was a trait people admired in her. She had always been averse to failing at any task which she undertook. According to the updated news broadcasts, the authorities were still without a suspect, a motive or a clue. To coin a phrase, they had bupkus.

CHAPTER FIVE

By early evening, the investigation had hit the proverbial brick wall. In a large conference room in the main police building at 750 Race Street, division heads, public relations spokespeople and those responsible for disseminating the ongoing information had all gathered. Police Commissioner Marty Sullivan, flanked by his elite team, stood in the front of the room. He called the meeting to order and a deafening silence filled the room.

"I would first and foremost like to commend each one of you in the ranks for the professional and expedient work you have shown in this investigation."

Spontaneous applause erupted, acknowledging his recognition for the efforts the force had put in. He continued.

"I needn't tell any of you the many implications this case has had on our department and on the city of Philadelphia. Nationwide coverage has already begun and we will all be subject to close scrutiny as to not only how we go about solving this case, but also by the speed in which we solve it. This city, like all other big cities, can ill afford to lose those dollars brought in by conventions and visitors to our businesses and hotels. We have seen a decline in homicides the past several years, as well as an increase in the rate of cases closed. We need to follow this trend."

Some self-serving applause went up, giving the Commissioner time to clear his throat and sip some coffee. He went on.

"Each of you at this meeting will be given various assignments and protocols designed to make the dissemination of all facets in this case more organized.

"With that in mind, I cannot emphasize enough that time is not on our side and this case needs to be concluded 'AFSAP', and for those of you who don't know what that means, it means As Fucking Soon As Possible."

Just as he was calling his deputy commissioner to outline what they had so far, a fresh-looking man entered the back of the room. Davis turned and smiled after recognizing the guest.

"Ladies and gentlemen, for those unfamiliar with our guest, I would like to introduce Agent Dieter Delano Treble. He is one of the Bureau's best profilers and was instrumental in helping us solve the horrific serial killings that plagued our city earlier this year. Just to let the truth be known, he really misses a good cheesesteak hoagie."

"Don't forget Tastykakes, too," Treble interjected, with tension-releasing laughter now filling the room. "Thanks for inviting me, Commissioner Sullivan," he added, along with a silent nod to his buddy Stephen Davis. He took a seat in the back of the room.

Deputy Commissioner Tyrone Mooring approached the podium. Tyrone, or Ty, as he was better known, was well-respected. He had begun as a street cop, earning numerous accommodations for his abilities and the way he embodied the new image of the Philadelphia police force. He was a bit intimidating for those who didn't know him. He was a broad-shouldered, well-built, African American man of six-foot-three. His piercing light brown eyes could either gain trust or intimidate, and the inflection of his spoken words gave him a definite authoritative air. He was a cop's cop and had earned the respect of all those he had worked with over his twenty-plus years on the force. He smiled his patented wide grin, nodding to some of his longtime buddies who graced the audience.

"I would first like to thank Commissioner Sullivan for telling it like it is and I am on the same page as to the high level of importance this case exudes. I will begin by telling you what we have so far as well as some of the assumptions we will be basing our investigation on. First, we just received word from the hospital that we now have one casualty and the two other victims are non-critical, thank God. We are basing our theory on that these individuals or the insurance companies they represent were the targets. Since there were three victims, we are assuming they were targeted as a group rather than as individuals. Ballistics reported that a round found at the scene is a Hornady Zombie max round which was probably shot out of a .308 rifle. Since it's a hollow point, we can assume that our shooter meant business and knows his firearms. Along the same lines, there were no reports of hearing the shots, which leads us to believe that a silencer was used or the shots came from a distance far enough away to be inaudible."

A hand shot up and was acknowledged by a nod of Mooring's head.

"So does that mean we know that the perpetrator is male?" a female captain asked in a non-feminist way.

"My apologies, Captain Parsons", Mooring countered, wiping away a drop of perspiration from his forehead, being slightly embarrassed for omitting the fact that sex was an unknown factor at this time. "Getting back, we have no witnesses who have come forward with anything pertinent. The team at our Crime Scene Unit is gathering any video surveillance footage that was available from slightly prior to noon and up until 2 pm. Our Computer Forensics Lab is in the process of gathering any threatening e-mails or hardcopies involving any threats made during the past several months."

The meeting ran for a little over an hour longer. Questions regarding tip lines, reward money and security for the remainder of the insurance convention were all asked and answered. The last area of discussion regarded the media, which was to be off-limits to all involved and would strictly be handled by the Public Relations Department of the PPD.

The meeting was concluded with all personnel returning either to their normal departments or home. As time progressed, hopefully so would a clearer picture of the events and the eventual conclusion to the case. This was why Treble had been summoned in, but only after a suggestion and brief meeting Davis held with Sullivan and Mooring. Weaving through the disbanding crowd, Davis and Treble tightly shook each other's hands and embraced in a man-type way.

"So, I only have you to blame for dragging me up to this crime-riddled city again, Davis," Treble chided, his tone bordering on the sarcastic.

"What a load of crap," he replied. "I know full well that you get the last word on where and with whom you spend your time," and they both smiled knowingly.

Davis continued. "And besides, you're a well-known figure and celebrity in this neck of the woods after such a stellar performance in the Titell case." The Titell case involved a serial killer who had been stalking women on the Internet. After meeting up with them, he brutally killed them, seeking revenge for the actions of his wife.

"Thanks, Davis, but you and your team also played a starring role in that case. How is your girl, Ashley Stone?" Treble asked in a sincere way.

"Great, and thanks for asking. Actually we just got back from five wonderful days in the Caribbean. It was both a much deserved and needed time out for the both of us. And what's up with you?" he inquired in his best Philly accent.

"After I left Philadelphia, a real interesting case popped up in Florida. This wealthy widow had been killed and they called me in to help figure out the killer. They had been pretty sure it was her ex-husband. The problem was she had four of them and we had to figure out which of the four it had been."

"Yeah, yeah, I read about that case. Turned out that two of the four were friends and they plotted her demise. Didn't one turn on the other or something like that?"

"Almost, my dear Watson. The truth was that the two suspects turned on each other and we made them both deals. Giving them twenty-year maximum sentences with time off for time served. But I've seen dumber criminals."

They both laughed.

"How about dinner tonight, or do you have plans?" Davis asked.

"As long it's not a cheesesteak," he replied. "I already had one and that's enough for one day. And besides, I don't know how long I will be here and I don't want to O.D. on them."

"Good, then Chinatown it is, if you are up for that."

"It's a deal, so let me freshen up back at the hotel and you can tell me where and when to meet."

"Sang Kee Duck House on Ninth and Vine Streets, say six thirty."

With that they both shook hands with plans to meet later for dinner.

* *

Julian Gando was spending this particular evening in a generic hotel in lower Bucks County, located northeast of the city limits. Serious precautions were being taken to guard the star witness in what was being hailed by the media as the fall of the east coast syndicate as we know it. The Philadelphia Daily News, known for its extra-large fonts and creative headlines, deemed the story *"Crime is on my Side"* in one of its more dazzling lead story headlines. He had been in protective custody for the past several months. Tomorrow he was slated to testify in the presence of the Grand Jury, leading to a likely indictment of three New York Crime bosses. The only stipulation was that he had to remain alive to testify in spite of the quarter of a million dollar bounty on his head. So far he had beaten the odds, thanks to decoys, leaked misinformation, and the creativity of the OCTF.

Julian Gando was antsy. He had grown up in the town of Hoboken, New Jersey. It was the birthplace of Frank Sinatra as well as just a ferry ride across the river to New York City. His father worked as a foreman on the docks. However, young Julian believed he also had his hands in something else very lucrative, because he often came home with presents to spoil his only son and their residence seemed nicer than his school classmates. He was very close to his mother, a stay-at-home mom who was involved in countless activities with the church. She doted on Julian and took him on trips into the city when his father was busy at work. When he was seven, his mom was expecting his much anticipated sibling; unfortunately, she miscarried at six months. They were all grief-stricken, but his mom never recovered from her depression and abruptly left her family and New Jersey and all the reminders of her baby, adding to Gando and his dad's devastation.

His father was much more suited to spending time with the guys than he was at child rearing. He was fortunate enough that his wife's sister lived in a close enough proximity to help out with the upbringing duties he so sorely lacked. His side job at the docks added extra income, which came in handy when slipping his sister-in-law some extra dollars for caring for his son. He was connected with the right people and those he took bets for trusted him not to skim a dime of their not-so-hard-earned money.

As he grew older, Julian appreciated the comfortable life style that surrounded him. He was not naïve enough to believe someone who worked in a manual job could achieve such a nice income, and the word amongst his schoolmates was that his father was a person not to be messed with. Julian liked that and received similar respect just because he was his father's son. In high school, coached by his father, he began to take bets on sporting events, and enjoyed the cash flow it was generating. Hell, no other seniors in high school were driving around in a new Camaro.

Gando continued his career in hustling and running around with those deemed "undesirables" in his neighborhood, but his demeanor was always friendly and respectful of others. He would shovel snow for his neighbors, lend out a few bucks, and always called his elders "sir" or "ma'am". All in all, he was a likeable young man in spite of the rumors that whirled around about his livelihood.

Just before Julian turned twenty-five, his father died in a freakish incident on the waterfront. Several tons of cargo were accidently released from a loading crane, killing him instantly. The investigation that followed classified it as a terrible mishap, and no one was ever held responsible. Julian was not as devastated as one might have expected, as he was becoming less dependent on and more distant from his father. He was now carving his own niche within the periphery of criminal activities, living in New York City and running with a group that favored brains over brawn. White collar crimes, such as penny stock scams and Ponzi schemes, yielded more money and cleaner hands. Through the end of the 1980's and into the new century, he was content and fulfilled with both the money and the security that his nonviolent scams brought in. And besides, he was never a fan of physical intimidation and vehemence, which always led to stiffer sentences if one were ever convicted.

His smarts and successes didn't go unnoticed, and, in the early 2000's, he was called in by some of the New York bosses to get involved in some of their more businesslike activities. In one instance, he was contracted to mediate and smooth over a dispute between several vendors, all competing for kickbacks in the restaurant industry. The competition in supplying food, liquor and linens, all necessities at fine dining establishments, was getting out of control. Gando was summoned to dole out various contracts to numerous vendors, making it well known whom he represented. There was enough of the pie to go around. Threats, violence and the destruction of property would only decrease the size of the pie, so he was called in to design an equitable arrangement for all parties involved. He not only accomplished this task but also added income, as well as set the stage for future "joint ventures." From that point on, he was called in by all three of the major New York families to settle disputes and solve any problems that arose. He was paid handsomely, gained much respect, and was able to choose which assignments he would take on. He had learned from his father to be respectful of those who wielded the power that could make or break you. Or even take your life.

Now Gando was on the eve of betraying those who had made him successful, those who now decided he was expendable and was no longer useful to them. They had tried to have him eliminated and they had failed. Frank Castro, Pietro Mancini and Salvatore Bracci, the boss of bosses, would now stand trial on a multitude of charges ranging from conspiracy all the way up to murder for hire. That is, unless Gando was unable to testify.

CHAPTER SIX

That evening, the local and national news was consumed with pictures, interviews and much speculation in regard to the day's events that had transpired in Philadelphia. Jaime poured another glass of liquid courage. For several hours since her return, she had been obsessed with watching the events she had put into motion. On another level, she was being torn apart by the moral implications of what she had done. She felt remorseful about the harm she had caused these sacrificial targets; they were real living people not directly responsible for her husband's demise. Conversely, she was hell-bent upon bringing attention to the injustices being thrust upon her and on those who had experienced similar circumstances; those who had lost a loved one or those who had been denied treatment after paying required premiums; or simply, those who had been ignored. These feelings were the ones that initiated her plan to right the wrongs that needed to be addressed.

Staring into Oscar's eyes, she said in an insecure voice, "I hope you still love me and agree with what I have done."

Oscar let out a deep familiar purr which Jaime interpreted as a vote of confidence.

She arose from the sofa, calling in Oscar and Cosmo, her remaining companions, for their dinner foods of choice. The dry cubed-shaped pellets tumbled into Cosmo's metallic bowl, initiating an immediate bark of approval. Oscar was treated to his favorite, tuna and cheese bits, which were emptied into a ceramic bowl with the words "Tuna Breath."

"I hope at that at least you two are on my side for what I have just done. I know it wasn't the nicest thing, but I do believe deep down it was the right thing, especially for your dad."

Neither gave any sign of approval, focusing only on what morsels remained in their respective feeding bowls. Jaime's feelings of guilt were continuing to ebb, her mind beginning to focus upon the next phase of her plan. Phase one seemed to have gone off without a hitch, and she needed to proclaim her intentions to ease the fears of the city as well as publicize her cause. There was time for that tomorrow. She was mentally and physically beat up. She arose and turned off the television before heading up to bed. Cosmo and Oscar joined her, being as loyal and non-judgmental as always.

****

Davis and Treble simultaneously arrived at the restaurant, the aroma of ginger and garlic filling the packed house, along with hanging ducks ready to be served to the mostly Asian clientele. Being a week night, there was no line at the door and Treble noticed his gastronomic senses and visual palatabilities now being teased.

"In all my visits to your city, why did you keep me away from this place? It looks and smells amazing," he said anxiously. The low level growl of his hunger pangs were also growing in excitement.

"Well, the longer you're here, the more weight you will put on. Philly really is a great restaurant city," Davis declared with some civic pride.

They were shown to a small table looking out onto Ninth Street. An army of waiters arrived with water, Jasmine tea, and glossy menus complete with illustrations of some of their more exotic dishes. Davis gave a brief synopsis of some of his favorites as well as some of the exotic dishes that were geared to native palates.

"I'm not really into the tripe or jellyfish, but if that's your choice, knock yourself out," he said whimsically. Treble's look of disgust indicated those choices would not even be considered.

After sipping some tea and studying the menus, they motioned for the impatient waiter to approach.

"Let's start with the roast pork and noodle soup. We would also like the roasted duck Hong Kong style and the salt baked shrimp."

The waiter nodded, finishing his jotting down the appropriate logograms, and vanished behind the kitchen doors. Davis initiated the conversation.

"If you ask me, what we have is either someone who is out for publicity, hates insurance companies, or hates the actors who represent them. Maybe a guy seeking headlines or just some sick psychopath," he said in a matter-of-fact cadence.

"Could be, but isn't it a bit early to jump to a conclusion?" Treble countered. "It could be a vendetta against one of the individuals who was targeted, or a headline seeker. And who is to say it's a guy, as you mentioned. Couldn't our perp be a female?" Treble added with conviction.

"A female?" Davis jumped in. "Aren't you the expert on these profiles? Name me one instance of a female serial killer who fired a long range weapon at a human target. I want you to name just one!"

"That means nothing. You know as well as I do that these homicidal sickos are always coming up with new twists regarding murder. And who is to say that it's not a woman who pulled the trigger?" Treble added. "Maybe she is ex-military, a hunter or just a gun enthusiast. Too early to say, Davis, it's just too soon."

The soup was delivered with impeccable timing. The conversation was heating up and lines were being drawn in the sand. Easing the oncoming tensions, Treble gave a look of culinary pleasure, commenting on how great it tasted. Davis agreed.

Davis continued. "Why the hell would some chick want to take a rifle, risk getting caught, and fire three shots at some harmless actors?"

Treble smirked before responding, finishing a spoon of broth.

"This is why we're called detectives, my friend. One pattern I have learned in profiling is that, at times, there is no pattern. Killers are reinventing the wheel all the time. John Allen Muhammad killed ten innocent victims ten years ago around Maryland. His goal was to disguise the shooting of his ex-wife. Why did he have to kill ten people?" Treble asked as his voice escalated, causing numerous head turnings."

"Still, I agree it's early, but it has all the signs of a random, senseless act which makes it even harder to solve. And I still believe we will find it was done by a guy who has some convoluted reason for his actions."

Treble took a deep breath. "Before we upset our fellow diners, let's just wait a while and see what comes of our investigation. Then we can argue some more and see who gets the 'I told you so' honors."

They smiled and agreed, both being competitive, smart case solvers and both hated to be wrong.

The waiter arrived with the main courses and the conversation waned to a minimum. After some serious eating, they began discussing unrelated topics, such as sports, vacations and social lives. Davis filled him in on his recent vacation with Ashley, gaining a nod of approval from Treble. Treble filled him in on his brief four-day Vegas fling, but had to sum it up using the "whatever happens in Vegas" cliché.

After the meal, Treble commented on how much he enjoyed it and told Davis that it warranted at least one more visit prior to closing the case.

"Might be half a dozen more, depending on how quick we solve it," he added, and they both chuckled.

Davis insisted on paying. Treble agreed and demanded the next one was on him, or at least on the FBI. They shook hands and made plans to meet tomorrow when more information was available for the investigation.

CHAPTER SEVEN

J aime arose from good night's rest. She was surprised how peaceful and undisturbed it was. She felt relieved that the previous day's events had subsided in regard to unnerving her. The two wagging tails at the end of the bed signaled breakfast time. Oscar, the more vocal of the two, crawled over the top of the blanket, giving head butts to Jaime's chin, evoking feelings of guilt for being too lazy. She jumped out of bed and asked the pair to follow. They did.

It was eight thirty and her week of vacation from her hygienist position, arranged in advance, began today. After filling the dishes for the hungry critters, she was startled by her cell phone ringing. Reading the caller ID, she noticed it was her good friend Meghan, or Meg, as she preferred. They had met at her dental office and, after subsequent random meetings, the two became friends. Meg was employed as a waitress in a slightly higher-end sports bar. Being well endowed went hand-in-hand with good tips, enabling her to attend bartending school. There was more money to be made serving drinks and she was tired of getting hit on.

"Open up, I'm on the way in," Meg said as she locked the car door and began the ascent to the second floor.

Jaime disconnected the phone and tossed on a robe as she headed to the front door. Before the bell rang the door was opened. Meg walked right by her and sat on the couch.

"Feel like taking a ride into Philly?" she asked as she removed a cigarette from her purse, offering one to Jaime. One of the things that Jaime liked most about Meg was that she was always herself, with not a drop of pretentiousness to her make-up. She flipped the lid of the Zippo, spun the wheel and held it out towards Jaime. She then lit her own cigarette, inhaled and sent two concentric circles of blue-grey smoke out through her lips.

"Very impressive," said Jaime, admiring the rings, "but why are you going to the city so early? Are you going to see…?"

"Yuppers," she said, cutting Jaime off, "Sid is only gonna be around till ten, he got some hearing or something to go to. And I'm working a double."

Meg was referring to her dealer, Sid, who supplied her with any pills or powder whenever she desired. She used it as a crutch, an excuse that she needed a lift to deal with her day-to-day existence. Jaime let her disapproval be known in the past, but the subject remained mostly taboo to keep their friendship amicable.

"Ya gotta slow down on that shit, Meg. Where am I going to find a friend like you if anything were to happen?"

"Advice taken, mom," Meg's response came with a hint of sarcasm.

Meg was five years younger and still in the stage where she felt indestructible and Red Bull wasn't cutting it.

Meg extinguished her cigarette, blew Jaime an air kiss and said she would check in later. Maybe they would grab a late lunch, she mentioned, as she walked back to her car.

Jaime did not want to procrastinate at the business at hand. She grabbed a bottled water, sheets of blank printing paper and sat down at her desk.

Her mind wandered in and out, focusing first on Jeffery and then back to the events that she had set in motion yesterday. This was Phase Two and it was just as important to complete this part of her plan with the same impact and success.

Her first thoughts turned to the method of delivery for her impact statement. She could not send an e-mail to the Philadelphia daily papers, or the authorities would be at her door in a heartbeat. The postal service was out, as it would take too long, and the impact of her actions would diminish. Then it came to her. She would compose a letter, buy a cheap laptop, send it from some generic restaurant with Wi-Fi, and then dispose of the computer. But first she must compose her letter and make sure that its powerful statement would be heard by all.

She began jotting down notes, highlighting the important messages she wished to convey, and then assembled them in a logical order. When she began to write, she noticed she had spent the better part of the morning on this project, but knew that it had to be perfect. She began.

To The American Public That I Am Proud To Be A Part Of, It is with the deepest regrets that a life was lost yesterday due to my actions. I am truly sorry.

My actions were intended as a reaction to the injustices and frustrations that many of us have experienced in certain regards. Let me explain. Several years ago, our government thought it prudent to come to the aid of some businesses that were failing during some tough economic times. Banks, auto companies and insurance companies were all recipients of our tax dollars redistributed by our government. The intention was to get the economy up to speed and productivity. Some companies reimbursed the banks with the money they had been given; others we are still waiting for. The particular focus for my actions was on the Insurance arena.

These companies charge exorbitant premiums, are stingy with service and totally arbitrary as to who is allowed treatment and when. Not only do we pay more and more each year for the privilege to be covered in our health benefits, but our services diminish accordingly.

Only five years ago, in 2007, executive salaries for these companies were out of control. According to Willis and Willis, the CEO of Travelers Companies made over 19 million dollars in salary, bonuses and stock options. Progressive made almost 5 million and Allstate came in slightly below 10 million. The highest compensated executive was from Cigna, and the total surpassed 30 million. Add on the funds paid for advertising companies, air time and bogus doctors on payroll to deny all claims, it's no wonder that our benefits are shrinking.

Someone must stop this abuse of our benefits, of our rights and of our ability to receive services that we pay dearly for. I for one am doing something about it.

Unless we, the American people, see some reform in this area, and see it soon, my actions will continue. I do not enjoy taking a life, but if that's what it takes to save hundreds of lives more, so be it.

I expect a written or media response to my demand within the next forty-eight hours or more reprisals will be made. Let us all band together to right this injustice so that we may live in a better world.

Peace is with us, as I am the Voice of the People.

Jaime read and reread her proclamation, making sure her message came over loud and clear. She was content that her message conveyed all of her feelings, that it would be well received by all those who read it, and that they too would agree with her principles.

Jaime saw that feeding time was long overdue. After stretching her arms to their full extent, she beckoned Oscar and Cosmo to follow, which they did with no hesitation. She would next throw on some clothes and the wig she had from an old Halloween costume, and purchase a computer. She did not want to leave any clues or trails, knowing that most stores' video surveillance rivaled that of any casino. She would pay in cash and fill out the warranty with a fictitious name. She zipped up her jeans, ran back downstairs and grabbed her bag and keys. Walking to the car, she waved at a neighbor pushing a stroller and entered the car.

After fifteen minutes, she arrived at the Best Buy, which now occupied an enormous strip mall, formerly the home of Garden State Race Track. It too was now a victim of suburban sprawl and the waning interest in the "Sport of Kings."

She pressed the key device to lock her door and headed towards the entrance. She walked by the security guard, who looked more like a bouncer than a package checker, and made her way to the computer section. Noticing that the two sales associates were engaged, she examined the lines of computers that displayed their prices as well as their specific capabilities. Not being totally computer illiterate, she found one that met the bare essentials of what she required. It was Internet ready, had sufficient storage and speed, and had wireless functionality. The box containing the machine was neatly stacked below the display. She removed it from the pile and headed toward the checkout area. She was thankful she avoided interacting with a sales person; that made one less person who could possibly identify her. At the checkout line, she was asked if she was interested in an extended warranty, which she politely refused. The total came out to slightly over three hundred dollars. She was asked if it would be cash or charge, and, if it was a charge, she could acquire a Best Buy card and save twenty-five dollars on her next purchase. Again, she politely refused.

With purchase in hand, she walked toward her car and let out a long exhale, relieving some tension that had been building. At the opposite end of the center was a Panera restaurant, which she knew to be Wi-Fi friendly. She pulled up in front and removed the computer from the box. She plugged the power cord into the lighter, enabling it to charge for a while. She exited the car and walked over to a local chicken franchise to grab lunch, as she hadn't eaten all day. When done, she returned to the car, noticed there was ample power in her computer, and she was ready to begin.

As she entered Panera, the aroma of fresh coffee aroused her taste buds and she suddenly craved - and thus ordered – a double espresso. With her beverage beside her, she booted up the computer and removed the note she had composed earlier that day. Then she Googled e-mail addresses for the USA Today, the Washington Post, and the two local Philadelphia newspapers, and entered them in the address line. She added the New York Times, the quintessential tabloid, as well. Why not go for the gusto?

She then carefully typed the message she had diligently composed, using Spell Check to confirm its accuracy. She made up an MSN screen name, *WeThePeopleFightBack@MSN.com*, and typed her manifesto. When she was satisfied with its content and accuracy, she aimed the cursor over the send button and clicked. An immediate feeling of accomplishment and pride filled her being. Phase Two was almost complete. She drove to the Cherry Hill Mall, looking for the large dumpsters that serviced the shopping mecca. She removed the hard drive and got out of her car. Then, making sure she was alone, she laid the computer down on the pavement, and drove over the machine. She put the car in reverse and repeated her actions, then put the car in park and retrieved it. She drove to the first dumpster in sight and deposited the mangled plastic and wires into the large metal bin. She would toss the hard drive into the Cooper River close by. She wondered how long it would take to see her letter on the news.

She arrived at the river in ten minutes, did the deed and headed home. Feelings of triumph and righteousness now engulfed her. She was eager to see what would follow.

****

Gando was dressed in his new suit, striving to look both professional and believable for his upcoming testimony. He had been briefed countless times on how to present himself as well as how to answer the questions he was asked. He was to be precise and offer nothing more than the prosecutors asked. For weeks he had been prepped, making sure his facts were both credible and true. This was a case that had to produce results, bringing down the largest crime syndicate in the country. He would begin at noon, admitting to the heinous murders he had committed and the reasons why. He would also include who had ordered them, speculating as to who had given the orders and for what reason. The federal prosecutor would lay the groundwork for a slam dunk. The three bosses would also testify, although he was expecting a rash of Fifth Amendment silence from the group. If he could cut a deal with the weakest link, the case would be done sooner than later.

After Gando finished breakfast, he was whisked off to 601 Market Street. It was south of City Hall and home to the U.S. District Court, Eastern District of Pennsylvania. There was more police presence en route than a victory parade for Rocky Balboa. Barricades lined the now empty streets, void of the media and any other living or breathing creatures. There would be no mistakes such as the one that occurred when Gando had turned himself in. Decoys and false leaks to the media had seen to that.

The well-armored military Hummer had pulled up flush to the back entrance and he was ushered in through the door. He was navigated by four vested agents toward the stairwell which had been under close scrutiny for the past several weeks. The elevators had too many moving parts that could be tampered with. A path was made to Room B. The door opened, exposing the Grand Jury room. It was empty of spectators, filled only with those chosen to serve or those who were just unable to beat the system and avoid their civic duties. On *Law & Order,* Jack McCoy tends to joke about how easy it is to indict a ham sandwich. In Philadelphia, it's tougher, as they have to indict a cheesesteak hoagie.

As Gando approached the witness stand, a loud crashing sound filled the room. Agents drew their weapons and the jurors ducked their heads on instinct. The one juror who did not duck nervously apologized for sending a pitcher of water crashing to the floor. The result was a slight easing of the tension that had consumed the courtroom.

In the course of the next four hours, Gando captivated the jurors, relaying the tale of how he first began working as an independent contractor for organized crime. He was called on to mend disputes between factions, clean up and conceal situations before they became headlines, and oversee nonviolent projects. He spoke with a slight New York accent, but the inflections and pace at which he spoke mesmerized those in attendance. He was an adept public speaker. Smooth.

He brought the room up to speed regarding the actions and events that landed him in his current position. He had recently been hired by the three New York bosses to pave the way for a rapid and efficient takeover of all Philadelphia and New Jersey criminal enterprises. He had no qualms about naming names, places or events that tied in the New York mob. He openly admitted that he had cut a deal, though the particulars of that deal were never mentioned. During his testimony, several questions were asked by the Grand Jury, all of which were deftly handled by the federal attorneys. When the time expired, they decided it would be necessary to continue the following day in order to complete his story before the votes would be tallied.

* *

During that same afternoon, the PPD and other agencies were busy continuing the investigation of the shootings that occurred the previous day. Assignments were being doled out and the legwork was in full swing. They had determined the caliber of the weapon and type of ammunition. It was now necessary to see where they were sold, follow up on recent purchases and check all those who had registered that exact weapon. Background checks were being done on the three victims, the two surviving ones coming out of surgery in stable but guarded condition. Michael Davis was searching the far reaches of the Internet, seeking similar shootings throughout the country. He was also in touch with insurance agencies who had received threats or hate mail over the past several years.

Dieter Treble was sharing a small conference room with several other profilers, hoping to provide an educated guess as to a viable suspect who would commit this type of crime. The group of five attempted to narrow down characteristics such as gender, age, occupation, background and education. Midway through the day and prior to an unexpected message, they had agreed upon several characteristics of their suspect. They were leaning toward the perpetrator being a male, although it was not unanimous, and in his thirties or forties. He was probably educated and somewhat intelligent, as he had not been caught. His action was probably aimed at the insurance industry and not an individual due to the fact that the victims were representatives of the companies and not executives. They agreed that more information had to be gathered from the victims and investigators. Interviews with residents were still being gathered as well as any videos that covered the immediate area of the shootings.

CHAPTER EIGHT

Although it had been early afternoon when the e-mail had arrived at its destinations, the information was withheld to release it first to those heading up the investigation. The respective tabloids were asked to hold back on the actual document until it could be better interpreted. They knew from experience that expediency of publishing or alerting the public to a criminal's demands and threats was a no-no. Whoever committed this heinous act not only wanted attention but also desired, as in this case, some type of social change. During airline hijackings and terroristic threats, negotiators were instructed to make trade-offs with the felon in order to get concessions, hopefully to end a tentative situation. This was deemed by the profilers to be the most productive road to travel.

✱✱✱✱✱✱✱✱✱✱✱✱✱✱✱✱✱✱✱✱✱✱✱✱✱

After Jaime disposed of the incriminating computer she had purchased, she stopped over at Wingman's, a newer addition to the old Garden State Racetrack property. It was considered a religious shopping experience by its loyal customers. It contained such amenities as a hummus bar, stuffed olive bar, six-dollar meal specials and almost any ethnic craving one may have. Her cravings were more simple. She picked up coffee, milk and Peanut M&M's, which she considered three of the five basic food groups. She added feta stuffed olives, Buffalo wings, and various choices from the fresh salad and grain buffet. She did maintain some semblance of healthy eating habits. After paying for her selections, she placed them in her cart and made a detour to the liquor store which sat cattycornered from the main market. She picked up a pint of Johnny Walker Red and a half gallon of some cheap chardonnay. She would be in front of the TV newscasts for the long haul and wanted to be prepared. She loaded her purchases into her Honda Accord and drove the short distance to her condo.

Upon her arrival, she carried the two sacks of groceries to the front door, unlocked it and deposited the bags on the empty kitchen table. She then went out the front door to get her mail from the bank of clearly numbered mailboxes. She flipped through the incoming mail as she walked back. She noticed a letter containing a return address from her husband's insurance company. This ignited an emotional fuse, which made her anxious to read the contents. She tore the seal off even before she entered her house, removing a plain white sheet of paper containing the company logo and a short note.

Dear Mr. Valle,

After careful consideration, our doctors have given their approval to proceed with the suggested procedures requested by your physician. We apologize for this delay and hope that your health benefits from it. We look forward to serving you in the future and wish you all the best. If you have any further questions or concerns, please feel free to contact me at the number in the top left corner of this correspondence.

Yours truly,

Jackie Tate, Claims Supervisor

As she crumbled the letter in her left fist, she felt her face grow warm, and an emotional anger begin to pulsate through her whole being. She was furious. She began to shake. She wondered how this form letter had reached her. Her husband had passed away almost a month ago, and she had received a condolence letter from the very same company several weeks ago, filled with no real conveyance of any remorse. She slammed her fist on the table as the tears began flowing at a higher rate. "Those bastards," screamed aloud as her body continued to shake in heightened anger. She turned and pulled the bottle of scotch from the sack. She removed a glass from the dish rack and filled it with several ice cubes. She poured out the caramel colored liquid until she realized she had drained a fair amount of the bottle's contents. She held it to her lips and took two large gulps, feeling a slight burn followed by a minor decrease in her ire. She grabbed a tissue from its box, blotting the subsiding tears, not caring about her running mascara.

She took a deep breath and headed to the living room. Using the remote, she pressed the red button and the 42" LED screen illuminated the room. She directed it to Channel 3, noticing the four o'clock news was filling the screen. Opening the large bag of M&M's, she popped a neon coated shell into her mouth as her eyes lay transfixed on the follow up story. The reporter, Tracy Tams, began.

"The Philadelphia Police Department, with help from several federal agencies, is continuing door-to-door searches and interviews in the area surrounding the shootings that occurred yesterday at the Constitution Center. With few leads to go on, they are also reviewing any video tapes or photos that may have captured any type of clue. The victim, whom most of us recognize as the awkward TV spokesperson for a well-known insurance firm, is not believed to have been the target of this attack. Neither were the two others wounded, one we know as "Flo" and the other who had been dressed in a green lizard mascot outfit. Both are recovering in local area hospitals."

The camera then panned over to a separate interview with one of those who had been stationed in close proximity to the lizard. He described the events that he witnessed.

"All of a sudden, yo, I see this red stuff coming out of the lizard's head and I know it's blood. Ya know what I'm saying, yo? I ducked down and tried to see if there was anyone shooting, but I didn't see nothing. Glad the guy is all right, and I guess I was just lucky, yo."

Jaime smiled a bit, being amused at the witness's account of the incident as well as his use of the English language. But she was disappointed and curious as to why her proclamation had yet to be broadcast. She wondered if they didn't take her seriously or if they were trying to get her to flush herself out. She would wait until tomorrow to take action. Also, it was still early and they might be saving it for the six o'clock news when there's a bigger audience.

Jaime was momentarily startled by a knock at the door. She wasn't expecting anyone this afternoon, she thought.

"Who is it?' she bellowed.

"It's me, Meg", the recognizable voice responded. "Open up, girlfriend," she added

Jaime got up and let her in, and Meg blazed past her. When she turned around, she noticed that Jaime's make-up was out of place and the whites of her eyes still had veins of red running through them.

"What's wrong, what happened?" she asked in a concerned tone.

Jaime led her into the kitchen, tugging at her hoodie to guide her in. After smoothing out the letter, she handed it to Meg and nodded her head, which indicated she should read it. She did. When finished, her arm dropped to her side and her expression changed dramatically.

"Those freakin' bastards," she said, almost mirroring Jaime's earlier comment. They just don't freakin' have a clue. Whoever did that shooting yesterday should be given a medal. They deserved it for what they did to you and others, too," she lamented philosophically.

They hugged momentarily and Meg grabbed a cigarette from her purse, offering one to Jaime. She pursed it between her lips, lit hers and held the flame out for Jaime. Jaime inhaled deeply, the nicotine giving some added relaxation in harmony with her scotch.

Meg pulled out a clear plastic bag and removed several pills from it, handing them to her friend.

"They're Xanax, and you look like you could use one." Jaime disliked most medications, including aspirin, but took one without much thought. She did need to calm down.

Meg extinguished her smoke, and, hugging Jaime again, said she had to go. They had called her into work that night because one of the waitresses had quit. What the hell; she had a good buzz and the money always helped. She said she would call later, and with that she was gone.

Jaime returned to the couch, noticing the crawl on the bottom of the screen that said "late breaking news." She dropped the candy and focused on the story. She was sure she now had been heard and she smiled.

The FBI had issued a "strong request" that news agencies should hold off on broadcasting the letter that had been received. The Washington Post, New York Times and U.S.A.Today had all abided by the request. But one paper in the liberal city of Philadelphia, the birthplace of independence, disregarded the requisition. While the editors were preparing the story for the early morning edition, a reporter leaked it to the local TV stations. The Bureau's pleas to the three major Philadelphia news stations were unable to block the reading of the e-mail that Jaime had sent. As a result, the authorities were scrambling behind the scenes to compose a rebuttal to the decree. They would have to address the author's demands, agreeing with some points, as well as promise that the accusations would be investigated.

Not to be upstaged by Philadelphia, the New York and D.C. TV stations also broke into the regularly scheduled programming with live readings of her statement. The FBI contacted the stations and demanded that they too be allowed equal time. They did not want to have any vigilante activities that would mimic hers occurring anywhere else. The FBI's rapidly composed response arrived quickly at the stations, and they requested that the primary anchor person in each city deliver the message. They complied.

"The FBI and Federal Government wish to address the recent story that has just been released. At this time, with top priority, we will be looking into all accusations leveled against the insurance industry. If there is a particular incident that the author of this correspondence is upset about, please bring this matter to our attention immediately. All criminal charges will be suspended until further investigation. Thank you."

Jaime had gained national attention, albeit anonymously. She also didn't buy the bullshit about dropping any charges, but it was a start. She would sit back for a while and see what transpired. She resumed watching the broadcast and popping her M&M's.

The profilers who had been diligently coming up with the suspect's characteristics now had more to go on. They were almost certain that this individual had been personally denied treatment for which they believed they were entitled. Or maybe it was a family member. In all probability, that individual passed away as a result; the suspect had gone Biblical, taking an eye for an eye. This person was also "sacrificing themselves," willing to pay the price for their recent deeds in lieu of whatever sanctions they may soon face. This meant that he or she had lost someone close and no longer cared what happened to them, or wanted to be a martyr for their cause. In either case the detectives could now focus on claims that had recently been denied, connecting them to individuals who had died as a result. It narrowed the field but would still take lots of investigating.

The story was the main focus on this particular evening. Even Nancy Grace commented on the fact that there are other ways of making one's voice heard other than murder. But was she right?

CHAPTER NINE

The jet black Escalade turned onto Main Street in the Brooklyn neighborhood known as DUMBO. DUMBO stands for Down Under the Manhattan Bridge Overpass. The area is one of the most exclusive and expensive residential areas in New York City, with condominiums selling as high as twenty million dollars. The towering residences give panoramic views of the downtown New York City skyline and East River. The old factories and warehouses have been replaced by residential lofts, hip galleries and gourmet eateries. Its residents are in the upper echelons of their professions, such as the legal field, corporate management or financial markets. Being an exclusive place to live is a gross understatement.

The black Escalade pulled into the driveway of one of the more majestic homes. The attractive young driver jumped out and carefully carried his wares through the front door of the Bracci residence.

"I brought you some of your favorites, father" Marco stated in the respectful tone he used when addressing those who were his senior.

His father nodded with a smile, accepting the square white bakery box wrapped in the familiar thin white cord. He opened the package which emitted a sweet and familiar aroma that stirred his senses. It was filled with as assortment of biscotti, colomba, pizzelle and mixed cannolis. His smile widened even more.

"Marco, my son, not only have I raised a respectful and successful son, but also one who embraces his traditions. Thank you."

Salvatore Bracci arose from his chair and, putting his arm around his son, strode toward the kitchen. He pressed a button on the coffee machine and patiently waited for his habitual morning espresso. Marco politely declined a cup, his generic Styrofoam cup from the bakery still half full.

Bracci patted his son on the shoulder several more times prior to the filling of his mug, and then led him back to the family room. The view was picturesque, as the morning sun glistened off the river and its mango colored streams filtered through the openings of the concrete towers that lined the opposing boundary of New York City.

They both took seats across from each other, a black lacquered coffee table positioned between them.

"Talk to me, Marco," Bracci began.

Marco twisted slightly in his chair, aiming for a comfortable position.

"I think the operation with Castro is just waiting on your final approval. I feel it better to keep you out of the loop so that you will be in the dark if ever given a polygraph. Everything and everyone is in place. All I ask is that you spend the afternoon with friends, not business associates, so that your alibi is solid. That's all you need to know."

The elder Bracci nodded. His nonverbal action indicated that he both trusted his son's planning and that he would follow his suggestion.

"I'm going for the Colomba," the elder Bracci said, removing the dove-shaped cake flavored with almonds and orange peel and baked in a delicate golden crust.

Marco grabbed a cannoli, licking the sweet creamy filling that escaped the shell, and continued.

"The project we are working on in Philadelphia is proving to be much more complicated. His location is being well protected and our people are not privy to this sensitive information. He is well guarded and we don't want to make ourselves too obvious. We are trying a few different angles and hopefully one will work," Marco diligently reported.

"Very good, son," Salvatore began. "I am very proud of you and if things do not work out in our favor, I am confident that you will take over with few disruptions to the company we have made so successful."

With the business at hand and the ongoing events reported, the two discussed matters of lesser importance, but still critical to the organization's financial well-being. No one in the Bracci family questioned the hierarchy of power, as they were all taken care of financially, and were respectful of the competence Marco had exhibited to his crews. He was a hands-on guy and proved that to all with his actions and words.

The two men stood up, each ready to begin the new day. It was approaching nine o'clock when the traffic would be easing up and plans would be going into motion. They exchanged good-byes and Marco opened the door, exited into the daylight and set his sights on the day that lay ahead.

✳✳✳✳✳✳✳✳✳✳✳✳✳✳✳✳✳✳✳✳✳✳✳✳

Gando was running through a tunnel buried deep beneath the New York City streets. It was dark and musty and the only audible sound was an oncoming #5 train burrowing through the subway under the streets of Manhattan. As he ran, bullets ricocheted over his head, adding even more peril to his predicament. The blinding beam of light that emanated from the lead car illuminated the tunnel. Two loud banging sounds then followed, waking him from his nightmare. He woke covered in sweat, a feeling that he had never experienced before.

"Yo, Gando, it's time to get ready for your day in court. There's some coffee and the paper in front of your door," came the voice of the guard stationed outside his suite.

He pivoted out of bed and proceeded to get his paper and beverage. He carried the tray into his room and placed it on the standard hotel desk that sat directly ahead. He sat down and noticed the eye-grabbing headline of the Daily News: *Flo*-**lateral Damage.** The page contained a picture of the semi-iconic insurance spokesperson and was bordered by two sentences that told of her wounding during a downtown sniper attack. Gando smiled, partially because of the creative headline, but mostly because he was sort of glad that someone was attacking the usurious insurance industry. He sipped his coffee and followed the story on page three. He then showered and went through the routines of the morning. Half an hour later, the door opened and his guards began the morning trek to the Federal Building. His testimony was to begin at nine sharp.

The following two-and-a-half hours were spent solidifying his murderous rampage, naming names, times and what he thought to be the reason for each killing. The federal attorney than summed up his story and answered several questions. When Gando's services were complete, he left the room and waited in anticipation for the decision whether to indict or not.

The wait was surprisingly short, which was usually a good sign, especially since it wasn't a Friday when people wanted to get home and begin an early weekend. They did issue an indictment. Charges would be filed as soon as possible, hopefully before the day ended. They had been forging ahead with the case, a bit over-confident of the hoped-for outcome. With smiling faces and several high fives, they left the building to start the paperwork.

Gando was shuffled off to a new location. His time would be spent in protective custody until the trial began. It would be several more months of boredom and inactivity, but it was part of his plea arrangement and he would be free after the trial. And hopefully he would be alive as well.

****

The investigation of the previous day's shooting put the city of Philadelphia on center stage, being a national news extravaganza. In 2011, The City of Brotherly Love was anything but that; it led the nation's most ten populous cities with a murder rate of almost one per day. This was all the more reason to solve the case quickly. The forensic evidence was scarce, not having a suspect to accompany the means and opportunity. The motive was pretty clear, thanks to the note that had been sent by the shooter. Detectives and federal agents were following a number of theories.

The number one focus was to research insurance claims and deaths over the past six months, hoping that the doer acted upon his or her impulses for revenge. Treble and his team believed it may even have been a recent claim. They also focused on the actual victims that were shot, doing background checks on personal and financial factors and interviewing those who might have a grudge. The third avenue was to investigate the three specific companies whom the victims commercially represented. Although the least likely, it was a possibility that the revenge might have been related to an automobile issue. Video tapes were still being reviewed as well as the license plates that were gathered in the area. Still, someone could have made it out during the commotion and confusion that blanketed the crime scene. They hoped it would quickly come together.

✶✶✶✶✶✶✶✶✶✶✶✶✶✶✶✶✶✶✶✶✶✶✶✶

Jaime was mesmerized by the extent to which the nation latched on to this occurrence. Reports focused upon the financial dealings of these companies and huge profits they reaped as well as exorbitant upper management salaries. Reports of complaints against the way these companies handled and responded to their clients also raised questions. You could hardly spend an hour in front of the television without seeing several commercials for insurance companies. They all spoke of large savings and expert service, but the fact was, the ads were terribly written, corny and stupid. At least that's what was starting to emerge from the media. Jaime thought that maybe her actions were forthright and could bring changes for the good of the public. But realistically, these companies had strong lobbyists in D.C., were big campaign contributors, and the products they sold were one of life's necessities. Everybody had to have insurance for cars, for homes and, most importantly, for themselves. They could all be termed necessary evils.

Her mind raced as she took in the news coverage. Horror stories of homes being destroyed by fire, weather forces, or floods with inexcusable delays in addressing the problems. Individuals needing medical care or maintenance services were interviewed; all told similar stories of poor service or incompetence. It seemed to Jaime, maybe in a convoluted or self-serving way, that her actions were being embraced by the public.

What she needed now was to figure out what to do next. Would she give it more time to see the reaction and possibly the actions of the insurance industry she targeted? Maybe she could send another letter containing more details of her end goals? Or should she just go about her daily life and wait? She would feed the critters, get back to the news coverage and then think some more.

****

Frank Castro wasn't so much a creature of habit than a home body. He liked to remain within the confines of his comfort level. He lived in Brooklyn as did his sometimes-partner, sometimes-competitor, Salvatore Bracci. It was in close proximity, near enough to be wary as well as concerned. The Park Slope neighborhood, in which he resided, was made up of old religious institutions with a varied mix of architectural and historic features combined with a diverse combination of residential and commercial attractions. Some of its notable residents include Bobby Fischer, Steve Buscemi and Tom Hanks. Its nearness to Manhattan with its low crime rate made it the number one ranked neighborhood in New York in 2010.

Castro didn't stray far from his residence or the small social club where he held court during business hours. The club was well protected and it was by appointment only, which added to its secure location. On this particular Wednesday, he was flanked by two of his bodyguards who could have been easily mistaken for New York Giants defensive linemen. They were both very observant of their surroundings, their eyes and memory being cognizant of anything that seemed out of place. Although armed with automatic weapons and wearing Kevlar vests, they had been fortunate in never having had to test either of the two. The three men walked abreast, Castro secured between the two large men. From the upcoming corner, they heard the distinctive screech of tires pushing their limits. The bodyguards tucked Castro between them. Seconds later, the loud escalating siren of a New York City Police cruiser came barreling behind the speeding car. As they passed, the two heavyweights determined that there was no danger and they resumed their gait and protective positions.

The sunlight sliced through the buildings, adding a slight warmth to waning autumn season. They approached the corner bodega, one of the neighboring businesses on the small side street that housed the club. As they turned in unison, two men sitting on racing bikes appeared. Other than the semi-automatic weapons they pointed at the trio, they fit in with the daily neighborhood's activities. Short, powerful bursts of deadly lead streamed from the two deadly weapons. The bullets easily found their targets, since the men stood only feet away. Before they could re-act, let alone remove their weapons, streams of burgundy and crimson liquids appeared from the victims, spraying out from the newly created entrance wounds. They collapsed almost simultaneously as passersby turned away, ran for cover, or dropped to the pavement. In less than ten seconds, the street appeared surreal as three bodies lay motionless and time stood still. The two men nodded at each other and began pedaling away from the crime scene, their heads focusing on the pavement alone.

It seemed like hours before the familiar, high-pitched police sirens filled the silence. In a matter of moments, a multitude of blue uniforms converged upon the scene. They were followed by the usual stream of EMS vans and then by vehicles sporting New York Press tags and window placards. There would be no need for the EMS personnel at this scene, as all of the intended victims lay dead and, surprisingly, no innocent victims had been wounded.

CHAPTER TEN

The news of the three killings filtered down I-95 in a timely fashion. Coupled with the soon-to-be-released federal prosecutor's news conference, which would name the indictments against the two remaining bosses, New York City would now become the new focus of national attention regarding its homicidal status. Even a gyroscope ceases to spin when there is no one there to pull its string.

That afternoon, bail was revoked for both Pietro Mancini and Salvatore Bracci, as expected. The New York media followed the events of both arrests, shoving microphones and yelling questions as each man was led away in handcuffs. They would be taken down to Philadelphia for trial, as that is where the murders they had been implicated in had been committed. New York was okay with that, as it would allow its own lawyers to build up charges on unrelated cases they had been working on for years.

Simultaneously in Philadelphia, Philly DA Jack Strauss flanked Marci Butler, the attractive assistant federal prosecutor who would be second chair in the upcoming proceedings. Since she was a Philadelphia native, it was believed that she had a home field advantage and credibility to the case. She approached the makeshift podium and addressed the media.

"The Grand Jury today handed down a number of indictments related to the recent criminal activities and murder that shook our city over the past year. Mr. Peter Mancini and Mr. Salvatore Bracci will face a number of charges in their upcoming trials. These charges include murder, murder for hire, witness tampering, racketeering, and attempted murder, just to name a few. Their bail has been revoked and they will await trial in the upcoming months. Lesser charges were filed against Mr. Julian Gando relating to these crimes, but many have been reduced as he has agreed to offer testimony against these two alleged crime leaders. Because they have requested a speedy trial as guaranteed by their constitutional rights, we expect the case to begin within the next several months. We will answer no questions at this time and will release information as our office deems appropriate. Thank you all."

With the abrupt and unexpected conclusion, the conference ended and the media was left holding, well, whatever.

Jaime was not amused as she watched this new story jockeying with her recent shootings for the top story of the day. Her spirits were quickly uplifted when a follow up story of the previous day's shootings began.

"Authorities are still investigating the recent murder and two woundings that occurred during the Insurance Outreach held at the Constitution Center. Although tight-lipped about the investigation, police claim they are following up on leads that may help lead to the arrest of a suspect. At this time, there are no persons of interest in this case and profilers are working to develop the personality traits of the suspect. Anyone with leads or knowledge is urged to call the number on the screen. The reward for the capture and conviction of this person now stands at $50,000."

Jaime sat back with a growing concern, wondering if they really had any substantial leads. She had been careful to a fault in order not to leave a single trace of her actions or presence at the crime scene. Replaying the experience in her head, which she had done numerous times, she shook off any fears that she had left any possible clues. Her confidence returned and any doubts she may have had vanished. She would wait it out to see how the pulse of public opinion swayed…or would she? She arose from the couch, poured a glass of wine and went into her office where her next plan would be developed.

✳✳✳✳✳✳✳✳✳✳✳✳✳✳✳✳✳✳✳✳✳✳✳

"I am so glad we took that time off last week," Stone said as she sipped her Appletini.

She sat across from Davis as they spent the afternoon happy hour at an out-of-the-way corner bar in Center City.

"You got that right," Davis replied, smiling as he lifted his glass for a toast.

It seemed like eons ago that the pair had been soaking up the Caribbean sun, drinking foo-foo drinks with umbrellas and spending passionate evenings undisturbed. Over the past two years, they had been actively involved in solving the Rick Grosse case, the Silk murders and the ongoing case of Julian Gando, the mob hit man who had baffled the skills of those investigating him. Now an anonymous sniper had chosen Philadelphia as the setting for making a statement and they were deeply involved in the investigation. And, although they loved the challenge and excitement of police work, a brief respite from high profile crimes was welcomed.

****

Stephen Davis' brother was becoming both intense and focused on his new career. Two decades ago, the very young and idealistic Michael had been wounded in the Gulf War, resulting in a spinal injury that paralyzed his legs and confined him to a wheelchair. Angry and futureless, he retreated into a shell while dealing with his issues. Stephen allowed him his space while patiently encouraging and emotionally supporting him. During Michael's rehab, the government had trained him in computer technology and used him as a consultant for special projects. One day, Stephen asked him to do a clandestine search that helped solve a major case. This ignited Michael's spirit and enthusiasm and was the turning point in his life. He soon became an invaluable consultant to Stephen and the OCTF and ultimately was hired as a full-timer. He was a well-respected force in his new position because of his computer expertise. Living on cheesesteaks and Diet Coke, he had come up with several good leads. A woman in New Jersey had just lost a loved one due to the incompetency of her health care provider. His policy had been suspended even though his premiums had been paid for the whole year. Before his benefits were reinstated, he collapsed and died. What made it even more interesting was that the woman was a firearms expert and local big shot in the NRA. Bingo, Michael thought, and relayed this information to the New Jersey State Troopers. Search and arrest warrants were quickly secured and authorities hoped that this was their shooter.

As the troopers approached the Roundhouse, Michael was getting high fives and kudos for the promising lead he had discovered. The media, camped outside the building, were thrusting microphones at the suspect as she was led in. Her head was obscured by a hoodie, her pace brisk to avoid the press. Two homicide detectives quickly ushered her upstairs to an interrogation room. There were two chairs in the center, a small desk for taking notes, and a third chair which she was told to sit in. The chair was backed up against the wall, pinning her into a corner. It was a claustrophobic arrangement, which is what they had intended.

She was Mirandized, offered a beverage and then asked if she understood her rights. She nodded and then loudly proclaimed her innocence. For the next three and a half hours, the tape recorder whirred as she answered all questions presented to her. Early on in the interview, she had given an alibi. She stated that she was still at work when the shootings had taken place. At that point, the medical office in which she worked was called. Since it was closed, the task of finding the owner or office manager took over an hour, but someone was finally reached. After her alibi was confirmed and they were convinced she had no involvement, direct or indirect, in the shootings, Carolyn Wise was cleared as a person of interest. Back to square one.

She was escorted out of the cinder block room and whisked downstairs to the exit. Two uniforms accompanied her, planning to drive her home as well as shield her from the hordes of feisty reporters that surrounded her. Captain Hawkins then informed the gathering that this woman was not a suspect and they should pack it up. That was all he said, passing on the opportunity for his fifteen minutes of fame.

Michael was disappointed but, instead of brooding, he went right back to the computer to check any incoming responses to his many queries. He had every intention of pulling an all-nighter and becoming an integral part in solving this homicide. He loved his new position and hated failing at any undertaking he attempted. He took another bite of his four-hour-old cheesesteak and clicked back on to his inbox.

****

Right now, his brother Stephen was more involved in carnal pleasures than in mentally stimulating ones. He had returned to his apartment with Ashley, probably consuming enough shots of Jack to propel him over the legal limit, so Ashley had taken the wheel. She only hoped he didn't have too much that would render his mechanism out of order. She would soon find out it did not.

She intertwined her fingers into his and guided him into the bedroom, with totally no resistance whatsoever. She led him to the edge of the bed. Resting both hands on his shoulders and sliding her foot to the back of his leg, she easily forced him to take a seat. She dropped to her knees, deftly undoing his belt, pulling down his zipper and removing his trousers quicker than Houdini. His boxers offered less resistance, except for the protruding bulge which stood at attention. Licking her palm, she began to rotate her hand from top to bottom, which added to his stiffness. At the same time she made circular motions with her tongue around him, making only the slightest of contact. He fell back on the bed as her speed and intensity increased. The sounds of pleasure he expressed did as well. Several minutes later he was appeared to be drained, both physically and mentally. She then slid up on top of him, softly kissing his neck. Out of nowhere, he reversed their positions, now being on top of her. His eyes looked into hers, conveying what he was about to do next.

He slid back, placing his feet on the floor, and returned the favor of disrobing her. Placing each hand on her thighs, he tilted her back until she was prone on the bed. His mouth covered her as his tongue made circular motions over her magic button. Almost as quickly as he, she reached orgasm, gently pushing him away as she also went into sensory overload. Actually and literally, they screamed. He eased up and threw himself on the bed next to her.

Their conversation was at a minimum as it was obvious their actions spoke louder than words. Ashley nestled her head below his arm, threw her left arm over his midsection and they slept contently till morning.

Part II

CHAPTER ELEVEN

During the past ten years, the weather in Philadelphia has been as unpredictable as a Philadelphia Eagles' fourth quarter. Over the past decades, the city had experienced 80 degree temperatures as well as massive snowstorms bringing almost six feet of snow in a week's period. The tough working class make-up of the city was more than adept at dealing with any type of adversity it was thrown. This winter would bring its share of much the same.

The high profile case of the two remaining mob bosses with the long list of charges was nearing its onset. Peter Mancini and Salvatore Bracci were to be tried together, as the charges were identical and they had the premier attorney, Ted Gussman, who was both quite flamboyant and undefeated. He had filed several motions in regard to the trial, winning the ones he thought important but losing on the bail hearing. There was no way, no how these two would be released on their own recognizance. He had succeeded in getting a motion granted that would force Gando to admit to his murderous acts, and would attack that as having been done on his own volition and not on a direct order. Gando was safe regardless, having cut a deal with the Feds that was just as secure as the vaults at Fort Knox.

During this period, the OCTF had been relatively peaceful, in large part due to the inactivity and lack of leadership in the organized crime arena. They were challenged, however, with a violent and greedy Asian gang in South Philadelphia.

The Red Dragons were making their presence known with their ruthless tactics. For several months, they had been kidnapping the children of well-to-do families, demanding six-figure ransom payments. Any hint of police involvement would cause the immediate death of their loved ones.

Through late fall and into early winter, about a half a dozen of these abductions took place. In each case, the families dealt directly with the abductors and the hostages were returned unharmed. The OCTF team members learned about this by sheer luck as they were dining in the Chinatown section of the city with an officer who spoke Vietnamese from his days stationed in that country; he overheard a conversation from the table next to them. After some not-so-subtle inquiries, he found a witness who had paid the ransom, felt safe and wanted to make sure no family would go through what his did.

A sting was set up to bring down the gang. A federal agent of Vietnamese descent was given a false identity. Word went out in the community that he was one of the largest investors of commercial real estate in his homeland and parts of the U.S. He was moved into a large townhouse on the waterfront and started to get into a daily routine that would be noticed. He was not only wired for sound but also under surveillance 24/7. In less than two weeks, after leaving his residence and clearly out of sight, a van pulled up to his home. Four men dressed in identical garb charged up to the door and gained entry. The only obstacle they stumbled upon was a half a dozen SWAT members aiming serious automatic weapons at them. The driver of the van was oblivious to his buddies' predicament and only realized something was amiss when two plainclothes officers approached the vehicle with their Glocks framing his head.

"Cuff 'em and stuff 'em," said one of the arresting agents, and the driver was not so gently eradicated from the vehicle.

After a short trip downtown and almost a shorter interrogation, the gang was arrested and charged with a laundry list of offenses. Since the previous victims had remained silent about their ordeals, it was only after this bust that the media ran the story, giving well-deserved and an overabundance of accolades to the OCTF and its assisting teams. Davis and the squad had become kind of media darlings to the residents of the city. In the past several years, they had solved many high profile cases, modestly accepting their tributes. Their wholesome looks and crime solving rate would have earned high Nielsen ratings had they been a fictional creation of Hollywood.

****

Gando had been getting restless during the time spent waiting for his ordeal to end. His pent up anxiety was sporadically alleviated with short trips to some of the spots he missed. He was treated to an occasional dinner of his choice and even went up to Philadelphia Park for a day of gambling and the ponies. Most of his ill-gotten funds had been seized by the government as part of his plea deal, but his monthly allowance had been building up due to his lack of activities and places to spend it. Besides, he still had two accounts with six figures that remained undiscovered. They were under fake names, and the well-forged documents that went along with those accounts were safe from discovery.

Every so often, thoughts of Bryant entered his mind, but more as pleasant memories than as a focus of revenge. Bryant Merril was the love of his life, the woman he loved more than life itself, and he accepted that it was his fault she left him. Gando was adept at putting things in perspective; he was a realist who weighed out all options and chose his actions on the theory of minimum risks that would yield maximum benefits. Except for the series of poorly analyzed choices he made that landed him in his current position, he rarely fucked up. All this idle time gave him adequate opportunity to weigh his options. He thought of leaving the country, but was not sure where to go. The West Coast was an option, but he had no friends or contacts out there. The New York, Philly and Jersey area was out of the question; the long arm of the organization he had betrayed had too many eyes in that region. Florida was becoming a more likely place to settle down in. Keeping a low profile with a new identity was at the top of his list. This was as long as he survived his upcoming testimony.

* *

Jaime had been going through a tough time. Depression over her husband's unnecessary death, some guilt over her ruthless actions, and the internal torment of what to do next tore at her daily thoughts. A month after the murder, she had sent a follow-up letter in the same manner as the first. She threatened the insurance industry with further actions unless serious changes were made. She demanded that lawmakers institute legislation that would prohibit these companies from denying benefits to those individuals whom their doctors had deemed "of a necessary and urgent manner." She said her timeline was firm and she would "make her voice heard again" if nothing was accomplished before the first day of spring. As winter approached its finality, no actions had yet been taken and no laws had yet been enacted. An occasional story of the unsolved case would be mentioned on page twenty, far from the main stories of the Daily News, along with news of insurance horror stories and the companies' lack of accountability.

In fact, weeks after her actions, a copycat killing took place in - where else - sunny California. An employee-turned-whistleblower was terminated several months before he would qualify for his pension and lifetime health benefits. His wife had been in critical need of a liver transplant and had been waiting for the right match. When the call came that it was now available and the procedure could be arranged, he was abruptly terminated and her name was dropped from the list.

During the following week, the employee, R.J. Raymond, purchased an automatic weapon capable of firing thirty bursts per minute. Armed with several magazines, he returned to his office and entered the claims department. He brandished the frightening looking weapon and drained all the ammunition. He was able to reload once before hearing the wail of distant sirens. Before removing his handgun and penetrating his brain with a fatal blast, eleven lay dead and six were wounded. The note found in his possession had quoted a bit of Jaime's letter. And yet, to this date, no policy changes regarding health care issues were addressed by, as Mr.

Raymond termed them, "greedy, arrogant executives, playing God, who decided who would live or die."

Public reaction was morally and ethically divided. Although many condemned the use of violent actions leading to the killing of innocent victims, others saw it as a call to justice, some even calling it a modern day Boston Tea Party, complete with some 21st Century blood and guts. In either respect, these two crimes were still in the public's eyes and even had been gingerly approached by some candidates during the past November's elections. Only time and the level of public tolerance would determine its future course of direction.

✳✳✳✳✳✳✳✳✳✳✳✳✳✳✳✳✳✳✳✳✳✳✳✳

Stephen's brother, Michael, had become a fixture on the dwindling squad of those assigned to what was now labeled the PhilKill case by some creative second-rate reporter. It was a term hated by the Philadelphia Tourism Committee. Since his brother was spending more time with Ashley, he and Dieter Treble were becoming friends. Treble was noticing a lot of his brother's good qualities in Michael. He also liked the role of mentor he was becoming to the inexperienced investigator as well as learning some neat tricks on the computer to skirt the firewalls and security programs that were elusive to him.

Treble and his team had worked and reworked their profile of the killer. The fact that no additional actions were taken, other than the brief note and time-sensitive threat that was still weeks away, left them at a stalemate. They had questioned over fifteen hundred possible leads, including individuals who had filed complaints with the Federal Insurance Office, those who had sent threatening communiques to specific companies, and those who had been denied claims which led to deaths in their families. The latter was by far the longest. They had also interviewed almost every resident in the area near the crime scene and ran every license plate they recorded. Each of these investigations yielded the same results so far: zilch, nada, zippo, bupkus.

That's when Michael came up with an idea, a plan that seemed so obvious, it made the others feel like rookies.

"Here's the deal," Michael began with a rising enthusiasm in his voice. "We can try to flush this son of a bitch out, bait him, if you will. You have a pretty good idea about this person's traits and flaws. We can put a response letter into this week's Philadelphia Inquirer like an open letter to our killer. You know all that psychobabble and how to get a response and…"

Treble broke in mid-sentence, finishing it.

"And if we goad them into another act of violence and more killings, then what? There are no guarantees that we will get that verbal response we are looking for. Let's put that idea on the back burner and just give it a little more time."

Michael and Dieter were extremely frustrated and everyone, the whole police force all the way up to the FBI, was clueless, although no one would admit it. Intermittent stories ran in various papers across the country, assuring the public that new leads were still pouring in and the investigation was in full swing. In reality, it was at a dead stop. Spring was approaching fast and, along with it, a firm deadline given by the sniper that more of the same would follow. What would follow? What all the investigators needed to make sure of was that *nothing* would follow and the case would be solved.

* *

Bryant Merril and Abby, who now had her name legally changed to Abby Road, grew closer. They initially met through Julian Gando. He occasionally conducted business with a special man in Abby's life, and she still blamed him for initiating a series of events that resulted in the death of this friend. Bryant had been absolutely madly in love with Gando until the night she caught him in, literally, a compromising position in Abby's upscale bordello. The ruckus she created caused a police response that ended with the arrest of Gando and the start of the on-going trial against the New York mob bosses. The tragic events over the past two years that they had shared forged the close bond of friendship. Both had lost loved ones, both now had a nice nest egg, and both were socially unattached. They were woman of leisure, spending time at the gym together several days a week, frequenting the hip clubs in the city, and even embarking on some great vacations. They had hit Vegas, not caring if everything "stayed in Vegas," cruised the Caribbean, and treated themselves to an all-inclusive stay in Jamaica.

Life was good and it appeared that neither would have to testify at the big upcoming mob trials, nor would any charges be brought up against them. During one of their post work-out lunches, Abby tossed out an idea.

"I spoke to an old friend yesterday, actually one of my old employees, Allie Medwick. Allie is in Florida and invited us down for a few days to Fort Lauderdale. What do ya think girlfriend?"

Bryant sipped her Pomegranate martini and winked. Raising her glass she proclaimed, "Here's to getting a Zone A boarding pass on our Southwest ticket!"

Abby smiled in approval and began to tell Bryant a little about Allie.

"She was one of my best. The clients loved her because she could role play almost any type of fantasy they wanted. She was extremely good at the rape fantasy fetish and the schoolgirl thing. She had a real innocent look when she wanted. Then she went and fell for one of her rich clients. That lasted for a couple of years. She quit, moved down to Florida, got married for two years and is recently divorced. You will love her," Abby promised.

"Let me tell you a funny story about Allie and her work," she said, trying to conceal her laughter as she recollected the tale.

"This huge guy, his name was Angelo Moroso, but we called him Angelo Morose, would only pay to work with Allie. He got off on her dressing as a schoolgirl, plaid skirt and all. He would ask that she smoked and cursed as she addressed him, and then he would put her over his giant knee and spank her. And he never even sexually got it on with her. She made a grand an hour. We used to have tape recorders and mini cameras in the rooms just in case things got rough. She wanted to put it on YouTube but was afraid of the repercussions." Abby never tired of telling the story and Bryant's laughter demonstrated her amusement.

"Ya know, Abby," Bryant began, "I've been thinking, about maybe moving down there. Good weather, the real estate market is a steal and we can set up a business. Oops, did I say *we*?" she half-heartedly corrected herself.

"*We* works for me" said Abby, confirming the growing friendship they shared, maybe even taking it up a notch.

They continued their luncheon of Cobb salads and martinis. They now had something to think about. They would book a trip after lunch and take things as they came. That's the way they were, not into making any definite plans and living life along with the curveballs it threw them.

CHAPTER TWELVE

The predictably unpredictable weather of mid-February in Philadelphia was at it again. The so-called "AccuWeather" forecast for the city, a name created by one of the city's news stations, would be more aptly dubbed "InAccuWeather," as far as today was concerned. The forecasters called for a high of 45 degrees with single digit winds and scattered clouds. In reality, the thermometer had reached almost 60 degrees by ten in the morning. The sun sliced through the buildings by the Federal Courthouse where opening arguments were to begin in the Bracci-Mancini trial. Maybe it was a divine signal that the guy upstairs would be keeping an eye on the outcome. The witty Daily News failed to disappoint, as the morning edition proclaimed **"Bosses Facing Losses."** It might not have been a Pulitzer winning headline, but it sold more papers than usual.

Those who had been instrumental in the arrest and aftermath of this high profile case were all in attendance for opening day. Davis's entire group from the OCTF was sitting up-close-and-personal, as was Sean Finnegan, their Atlantic City counterpart. Treble was also there, taking a respite from his ongoing sniper investigation. Abby and Bryant were absent, feeling no need to stir up past memories or animosities. Several of the murder victims' family members were present. Bernadette Madison, daughter of Atlantic City victim Johnny Pudello was there; he was brutally shot during an upscale party he had thrown for himself. She was his only child and truly a "daddy's girl." A smattering of the other victims' families was also there, both out of respect and in their need to see justice prevail.

Both Bracci and Mancini's sons were there, showing support and solidarity of the two crime families. They sat at opposite ends of the back of the courtroom. Although they were in the minority as far as hoping for an acquittal, they were totally untrusting of each other, even though their fathers were facing similar fates. And Mancini's son, Aldo, known more commonly as Al, wouldn't put it past Bracci to have his father silenced, just as Castro had recently been.

Precisely as the clock struck ten, Judge Judy Putman tapped her gavel three times and called the proceedings to order. The press was gentle on Judge Putman, limiting their comparisons to the illustrious judge on television. Her appearance was quite different as well. Standing at 5'8", she was a head taller than her counterpart. Her red diva-styled hair and warm brown eyes showed both a passionate and stern side to the woman. She was known as a fair judge who took a more conservative approach to the law and its amorphous limitations. When all were seated and the noise decibels were at a minimum, she spoke.

"The United States District Court for the Eastern District of Pennsylvania is now in session. We will be hearing the case of the United States versus Mr. Salvatore Bracci and Mr. Pietro Mancini on the charges of murder for hire, racketeering…"

She read nearly a dozen more charges, most relating to the Racketeer Influenced and Corrupt Organization Act, or RICO, which had been passed by Congress in 1970. In essence, anyone convicted of committing two of the thirty-five crimes contained within the statutes can be prosecuted under RICO. The act not only offers stiffer sentences but also can be used as a bargaining tool to move up the food chain. Since the two men on trial were the top of the chain, the proverbial buck would stop here.

Judge Putman then asked the prosecution to begin its opening. Gerry Brett, the Federal Prosecutor, was a fiftyish, well-dressed man. His boyish good looks and laid back style were probably his best attributes. He was often taken a bit too lightly by many defense attorneys. By the time a case had been argued, they were usually second guessing themselves and coming out on the negative end of a verdict. Brett loved the game of law and was one of the most successful attorneys in the Federal system.

He circled around to address the jury with a gait of commonness and confidence.

"Good morning, ladies and gentlemen," he began his tone both affable and cordial. "The United States of America would first like to thank you all for taking time from your work and families to be a part of doling out justice to those who are in business to circumvent our laws."

Ted Gussman stood and immediately objected, saying that no one had been convicted of any crime in the two minutes since the trial began. Sporadic laughter dotted the room, which was met by both a gavel bang from Putman and a ruling of "sustained," but Brett had made his point.

Brett smiled and apologized, continuing his opening without missing a beat.

"The people would like to present the facts as we see them so that you will all be able to make a logical and responsible decision. The two defendants sitting here today are accused of a number of criminal activities, all quite serious in nature. Let's examine our case."

For a good part of the morning, Brett constructed a timeline along with the illegal events that occurred in those specific periods. Because of Gando's full cooperation and steel-trap memory, the task was easy. He took them through Gando's decades of work that he was contracted to do as an employee of the defendants. He then became more specific, starting with the meeting in North Jersey, the killings in Philadelphia, the hit in Atlantic City, and the business plan on the future expansion into the area south of New York. His presentation and staging could have been nominated for a Tony award. His eye contact, the inflection in his voice and his movements were well orchestrated, holding the jurors' undivided attention. He handled all objections and interruptions that Gussman threw at him with both wit and professionalism. He was winning over the jury in a captivating style. It was almost as if he owned them.

Gussman was not to be outdone or intimidated. His expensive suit and slicked-back hair portrayed him as a player. This was maybe not the best choice, as his clients were not the most popular kids on the block.

But he was also a showman and loved the media hype and exposure. Several years back, he had defended two teens accused of murdering the seventeen-year-old girl's parents and then undertaking a drug-crazed road trip. The girl denied any participation, using the defense that she was in shock and was a helpless victim of being kidnapped. That argument was quickly dismissed when the prosecutors saw a video of her skipping into a convenience store to buy cigarettes while her supposed kidnapper filled his tank with her parents' credit card. The best he could do was a thirty year mandatory sentence with little hope for early parole.

Gussman deliberately feigned thinking as he approached the jurors, his right hand stroking his chin and head slightly tilted downward.

"Ladies and gentlemen, I would first like to say that I agree with my esteemed colleague that I too appreciate your willingness to participate in your civic duty. I know it's a strain on your daily life, but you all are doing the right thing."

During that brief soliloquy, he made a conscious effort to make eye contact with each member of the jury as if it would help him read the minds of each to figure out how he would win their votes of acquittal. He continued.

"What I will be attempting to demonstrate is that this case is highly circumstantial. It all boils down to a he-said-he-said type of case. For one thing, there are no connections to these individuals, such as cell phone records or taped conversations. There is no forensic evidence such as fingerprints, DNA or documents that prove my clients were in any way involved. Both of my clients have air tight alibis for the time each of these horrific crimes was carried out. Guilt by association is not grounds for a conviction, and I will prove that this is what these charges consist of."

His tone was sedate and his voice steady. He used his hands to emphasize his points and everyone in the court could see that he had their undivided attention. It was becoming apparent early in the proceedings that these two orators were quite evenly matched and the outcome would probably be in doubt until the final slip of paper was handed to Judge Putman.

Gussman filled the rest of the morning iterating each of his points while dismissing the groundwork that had been so artfully laid out by his adversary. His style never varied; he was even-tempered and direct in every point he clarified. Like two Roman gladiators, these two were evenly matched in tactics and smarts.

Gussman ended just before noon. The judge then suggested a recess for lunch, with witnesses to begin their testimony at the start of the afternoon session. As the well-worn cliché goes, let the games begin.

CHAPTER THIRTEEN

Abby and Bryant sipped their coffee and indulged in an order of spicy Buffalo wings as they waited at the airport. They had secured Zone A as they had hoped and would soon be boarding their flight to Fort Lauderdale.

"This vacation is soooo needed," Bryant said. "I need a big-time escape and I have never been down to that part of Florida, other than my parents dragging me down to Disney," she jokingly concluded.

"It will do us both good, especially since we don't have to listen to all that babble about the trial. I couldn't give two shits about it." Bryant had convinced her that she had rid herself of Gando's hold and she pretty much had. But some feelings were still there and she didn't wish anything that bad for him.

"You will just love Allie," said Abby, changing the subject before her friend began to dwell on past memories.

"Let's do a shot before we board. It's on me." Bryant stated in a way that precluded any objections.

When the shots of Ketel One arrived, they clinked their glasses and downed the double shots in record time, signaling the beginning of their soiree.

They boarded early, procuring boarding passes labeled A28 and A29. The tossed their carry-ons above their seats and took row 7, middle and an aisle seat. The 4:34 departure looked to be on time and would arrive just before 7:00 pm. Allie would pick them up and deposit them at the Harbor Beach Marriott Resort and Spa.

The flight was uneventful except for the guy in the window seat who talked in his sleep. It made the women laugh, especially when he called out a guy's name.

They touched down in Florida, ending the easy flight. Following the signs to baggage claim in a little more sober frame of mind, they waited only ten minutes for their luggage. Abby then texted Allie, who said she would meet them at area C in two minutes. They wheeled their belongings out to the curb just as Allie pulled up in her Lexus SUV. She flew out of the car and gave Abby a big hug and air kiss. They exchanged sincere smiles, and Abby introduced Bryant, indicating she was a great friend and not one of her ex-employees. That was all the information she needed to know.

Allie opened the cargo door and the ladies tossed in their luggage. Abby took the front seat and Bryant the back. They chatted like schoolgirls as they sped down the interstate toward the hotel. Allie suggested they freshen up and then run out for a quick bite if they were hungry. They agreed and shortly arrived at their destination.

They checked in and went to their room while Allie headed to the bar for her Long Island Iced Tea. Twenty minutes later, Abby and Bryant joined her, quickly ordering their cocktails. Taking turns, they caught up on their current situations, told some old stories and plotted their activities for the next couple of days.

"There is this great Happy Hour not too far from here. You two will love it. Lots of hot asses to look at or whatever," Allie said with a suggestive grin.

"Sold," Bryant said, the quickness in her reply surprising Abby a bit. After all, she was not quite a cougar on the hunt, but she was on vacation and could do whatever she damned well pleased.

"I do want to show you my store. It's called Toys O' Joy and you can't even imagine all the great stuff I have in there. Since *Shades of Gray*, business is way, way up," she said excitedly. "You can see for yourself tomorrow after brunch!"

The girls were feeling the effects of their flight and alcohol consumption, so they decided to eat at the bar. They ordered some appetizers, two more rounds of drinks, and said their good nights. They would rendezvous at eleven the next morning.

****

Morning came with the expected dry mouth and slight headaches. They showered, put on their make-up and took the elevator down to the lobby. Allie was punctual, as she had been the previous night. The ladies enjoyed their brunch at the resort's ocean view restaurant, savoring a wide selection of fresh tropical fruits, an assortment of pastries, and two pitchers of mimosas. Allie then herded the duo to her car, eager to show them her store. They drove for about twenty minutes, arriving in an average-sized strip mall. Toys O' Joy took center stage as the central store in the dozen or so businesses. She excitedly ushered them in for the tour.

As the trio entered the store, an immediate explosion of perceptions engaged the first timers: the sweet smell of an array of gels and lubricants; the distinct smell of well-tanned high-end leather goods, appearing in an assortment of distinctive items. These included face masks, body suits and various restraining devices for the dominating type. Their spectrum of colors ran the gamut from Flamingo Pink to "Spiderman" red to realistic flesh tones. While Allie observed their reactions, she remained silent as Abby and Bryant took in the vivid landscape. One of the sections was devoted to videos and how-to instructional tapes. Another featured mannequins displaying the latest in BDSM and revealing fashions.

Life-sized cardboard cutouts of well-exposed porn stars endorsing various products greeted them at almost every aisle. Belladonna's breasts and Katja Kasslin's cleavage grabbed one's attention at almost every turn. If aliens were to send an expedition, they would surely turn back and leave as quickly as they had arrived. No one would mess with creatures like those on display.

"Say no more," commented Allie, noticing the combined silence and awe the pair exuded. "You two look like kids entering the main lobby at F.A.O. Schwartz on Fifth Avenue for the first time."

When no response followed, Allie let the two explore her products with no tour guide.

"You have come a long, long way from your Philly days," chided Abby, following her statement with a wink and smile.

"You always said I was the best, girlfriend."

The three women met at the counter containing a wide selection of self-pleasuring devices. Hanging on the wall was an eye-grabbing placard that stated, "Who needs a man when you have a fresh pack of Duracells?" They laughed harmoniously. The array of products ran on electricity, batteries, solar power for the backyard enthusiasts, and one even plugged into a car's cigarette lighter. Upon closer inspection, they noted its pink flowery packaging read, "Driving with Ms. Daisy."

After touring the shop, they felt like they needed a cigarette. Instead, they decided to regroup and meet at five for happy hour at one of the new clubs on the waterfront. Allie said that if you couldn't find what you wanted or needed there, they could always come back to the store and settle for less. On that note, they piled back in the Lexus, Allie letting her assistant, Kitty, man the storefront.

****

After prettying up, the two guests invited Allie to their hotel room for some pre-dinner drinks and girl talk.

"You guys are gonna love this place. It's on the water, serves awesome martinis and there are plenty of tight-assed guys. Surprisingly, it's pretty down-to-earth and not too stuck up," Allie explained, washing her Patron down with a lime wedge.

"How long have you been here and managed to keep that Philly accent?" Abby asked as she followed suit with the lime.

"Long enough to know I enjoy it a lot more than Philly: the weather, this is a young area and the housing market is coming back. That's why you two should consider joining me."

Allie poured another shot into the three empty shot glasses and continued, noticing a hint of interest had been ignited.

"The store next to me is moving to another location as their lease is running out. A chic clothing store, maybe some spa services, the legal kind of course, or an upscale teen clothing boutique would fit in nicely. And I couldn't possibly do it alone."

Allie was on a roll, the "I-can-sell-ice to-an-Eskimo" roll, and she had their undivided attention. Little did she know the two had been considering a move but had remained silent about it. At this point they told her of their considerations and agreed to discuss some possibilities sooner than later. Tonight they were in party mode and business could and would wait.

Allie picked up the valet ticket and the trio was ready for whatever came next. They each had a cigarette while waiting for the valet, each seeming to be lost in thought. The car arrived, their doors opened, a tip given and the night was officially in play.

They arrived at "Oceans in Motion," the hot new aptly-named club. There was an outdoor deck, complete with a border of sofas, each framed under a collapsible canopy for privacy and whatever. There was a small indoor restaurant serving tapas, sushi and appetizers. An adjacent room sported a disco-like dance floor, the ceiling mimicking the night sky with flashes of thunder, shooting stars and an occasional UFO.

The ladies opted for an outdoor three top table with a panoramic view situated almost in the middle of the club. It was the perfect spot to both observe the patrons as well as be observed. Their drinks flowed almost as fast as the waters that sank the Titanic did. Just then, Bryant's eyes locked in on a young thirtyish surfer-looking type. He had green khaki cutoffs, a Rugby shirt and bronzed skin. This meant that he worked outdoors or didn't work at all. Abby waved her hand in front of Bryant's face, momentarily blocking the view. She shot a curious look at Bryant and threw her a question.

"Yo girlfriend, if I may ask. It's none of my business but is that guy also your type or are you just looking for an RH?"

Puzzled, Allie mentioned she was unfamiliar with that term. Bryant quickly answered and indulged her curiosity.

"It stands for revenge hose, which is what occurs when a relationship ends, you are pissed at the opposite sex and only want to get laid, which makes you feel like you got even."

"I love the term and the concept," said Allie. "With that term you can rationalize anything you want with no guilt attached. Next drink is on me."

In uncharacteristic fashion, Bryant pushed back her chair and headed over to her prey in a not-so-straight line. When she arrived, it seemed that he was glad she did, and he guided her by the elbow to his seat at the crowded bar.

"Gee, Abby, she sure fooled me. I didn't think she was the slutty, out-to-get-laid type."

"On the contrary; this is a surprise to me."

Abby went on to give an extremely abbreviated version of her relationship with Gando from the onset to the present. She omitted some of the criminal details, telling the story from a woman's point of view, making it easier to accept.

"And besides, I think a one night stand would do her some good. She needs it both to build up her confidence as well as to have some fun. She was hurt pretty bad and this might ease some of the pain."

Allie knowingly nodded and silently rooted for a climactic outcome in the literal sense. Just as the two got up to find the ladies room, they saw the couple head towards them. Bryant's sense of balance had diminished even more. The four met in the middle as Bryant made some brief introductions. Allie asked the guy for a business card or some ID. She was not with the sex police but rather was a good friend who wanted to make sure that nothing violent or extreme would happen to Bryant.

"Gladly," he said, mentioning that he understood her concern and what a good friend she was for taking such measures.

"I have never been on Americas Most Wanted, have no prison record and here is my cell phone so you can copy my number."

"Thanks for understanding and being a sport. You're okay with us," she said smiling. And, with that, the party was down to two.

Hearing an approaching vehicle, she removed her weapon and lay prone in the grass. After no one approached, she determined it was a false alarm. The same scenario repeated itself three more times and she was beginning to wonder if she should adopt a more detailed plan.

Jaime was growing impatient again, a new trait which had begun to consume her after the death of her husband. As it was nearing six o'clock, she returned to her car and decided to go home. Tomorrow was another day and she still had several weeks before the first day of spring and her threatened deadline. As she drove out of the neighborhood, she spotted Kim. She was alone and appeared to be heading home. Without thinking, she swung the car around and trailed at a safe distance behind so she would not be spotted.

✳✳✳✳✳✳✳✳✳✳✳✳✳✳✳✳✳✳✳✳✳✳✳✳✳✳

The trial continued to capture major headlines and national attention. Jane Valez-Mitchell and Nancy Grace were having a field day as the HLN network's ratings soared and the legalese flourished. Since any live coverage had been banned, only second hand reports and the artist's renditions of the scene were available. Julian Gando's testimony had set the stage. The prosecutors had contended that his actions were direct orders from the defendants. Since there were no phone records, a paper trail or any eyewitness accounts, it was coming down to which testimony was more believable. With a two against one ratio, Mancini and Bracci's testimony versus Gando, the outcome would be unpredictable until the verdict was in. This factor was probably the one that kept Bracci from whacking Mancini and lowering the odds.

On this day, the prosecution had rested and the defense was to begin its case. The defense attorney would focus on the belief that Gando had acted alone, both out of greed and the quest for power. They would stress the fact he cut a deal, knowing full well that it was only to save his ass and pass the blame to someone else. A long parade of character witnesses would testify that the two defendants were no longer involved in criminal activities and were running legitimate businesses. It was still unknown who was ahead and, more importantly, if the defendants would testify, although it was highly doubted. But courtroom proceedings were about as predictable as a Super Bowl winner after week one of the season. The trial was now about half through and as the cliché goes, "it's not over till it's over"

****

Jaime waited a few moments after parking the car adjacent to the open field. She removed her coat and pulled a camouflage hoodie over her head. She picked up the weapon case from the back seat and grabbed the Snapple bottle of Peach-Passion fruit she had just finished. The night canopy was now forming in the wintery sky and darkness would descend, aided by the new moon. She walked slowly through the knee high grass, which aided in making her footsteps inaudible. She grew a trifle nervous because this plan was more impulsive and less thought out than the first. Her emotions pushed aside her logic as she went into hunting mode.

Jaime returned to her spot and lay down, splaying her legs and assuming a prone shooter's position, which was second nature to her. She pulled more of the tall grass away from its roots to improve her line of vision. She was about twenty yards from the back porch. It was actually a large cedar deck, decorated with hanging plants, planters on the railing and symmetrically arranged patio furniture. She watched and waited.

Several minutes later the back lights came on, illuminating the deck in shades of ivory, red and blue. How patriotic, she thought, amused that this woman was working for a company that mistreated and ripped off the hard working Americans who supported her lifestyle. These thoughts helped her rationalize that what she was doing was the righteous thing. It would make pulling the trigger both an ease and a pleasure.

Through the sliding doors, she noticed the woman pacing in the kitchen, talking on the phone. Jaime thought it might have been some type of sign from above, since the vertical blinds on the large sliding glass doors were open, exposing a clear and unobstructed view into the kitchen.

Not wanting to risk the chance of the projectile's accurate path being misdirected, she went to Plan B. She grabbed the Snapple bottle, rose to her knees and threw an accurate Eli Manning-type screen pass that crashed against one of the large clay planter pots that decorated the deck. Seconds later, the distinctive click of the sliding door opening alerted her to resume her prone position.

As the door opened, Jaime could faintly hear fragments of Kim's phone conversation. "..Noise in the yard…probably raccoons…thanks, bye," followed by her sounds of displeasure. Her hands were on her cheeks and her head was shaking from side to side, displaying a look of helplessness, just like the look Jaime had after hearing of the insurance company's denial of Jeffery's claim. Kim's hands come down, but her head kept moving. The next move she made was to try to brush off the red dot that was now illuminated on her chest. She brushed at it and it disappeared, but she didn't know that it was now on her cheek. That was the last movement she made prior to helplessly falling face-first to the patio deck.

Jaime quickly arose but walked at a normal pace, crouched low, as she headed to her car. There was no need to check her prey. Jaime was as accurate as could be and the only thing left for Kim would be services for her last rites.

preferred to err on the side of caution. Several moments later, the sound of an emergency vehicle broke the silence of the early March serenity, and a flood of multi-colored beams pierced the darkness.

Several police vehicles, two EMS vans and a fire truck all converged upon the perimeter of the open field. Two men trotted out of the ambulance with a stretcher, and then doors of the fire truck opened to allow a gurney to be lowered, just in case the victim's condition was less than critical. It was not.

The Crime Scene Unit had arrived and was already cordoning off the area with the recognizable black and yellow crime scene tape. Some of the investigators concentrated on the surrounding open area, while others spread out around where the body was found. The coroner noticed what appeared to be a bullet entry between the right eye and the bridge of the nose. The size of the wound indicated that a large caliber projectile had caused an almost instantaneous death. The body was void of any vital signs and was hoisted to the gurney for a trip to the morgue for an immediate autopsy. Both township and state police collaborated and would start an immediate investigation. They already had learned the name of the home owner and would contact the next of kin for a positive identification. Pairs of officers were dispatched to begin canvassing the area for potential witnesses and background information.

After several hours of interviews with the neighbors and the crime scene investigators scouring for clues, the area was again tranquil except for the memories and headlines that would surface tomorrow.

CHAPTER SEVENTEEN

As the sun struggled to make a brief appearance, Jeff Ryan, a New Jersey State Trooper with the most homicide experience, was put in charge of the Medford Murder, as the Burlington County Times dubbed it. The body was now undergoing a thorough autopsy while his group was picking up the pieces. No shell casings had been left behind, indicating the killing was probably thought out. Score one for premeditation.

He and several other men were combing the field when one noticed that part of the tall grass had been flattened down. They did a small grid search but found no trace evidence. Whoever committed the crime was either an experienced pro or just plain lucky. But that's what police work is all about.

They had a little better luck on the deck. They were able to dig a fair portion of the projectile from the cedar siding on the deck. It was still mostly intact and the forensic guys would be able to identify the caliber and type of bullet. They could see if the bullet matched any other cases. If so, and if the cases were still open, they would be able to tie them together. Several hours and half a dozen cups of coffee later, Ryan seemed satisfied that they had uncovered all of the evidence and the investigation could begin. With the interviews from the neighbors, they would get back to the station and begin developing the scenario of the crime and eventually, and hopefully, would have the case solved.

✳✳✳✳✳✳✳✳✳✳✳✳✳✳✳✳✳✳✳✳✳✳✳✳

Back at the Roundhouse, Jim Kelly and Michael Davis were putting together the day's activities. They had interviewed over a hundred people whose license tags had either been caught on camera in the area or had crossed the Ben Franklin or Walt Whitman Bridge within a half hour after the shooting.

"This is getting old, quite old, Michael," Kelly stated in a drone and bored voice.

"Couldn't agree with you more," Michael lied, having yet to develop a hard skin and sarcastic attitude toward the boring grunt work more commonly known as 'following all the leads.'

Today they would cross the Delaware River, unlike the way George Washington had, and conduct some interviews with those whose tags had been recorded by camera.

The first stop was a Mr. Rich Mitchum, who owned a landscape business in the Garden State. When they arrived at his Cherry Hill rancher, he was in the backyard grilling some afternoon burgers and bratwurst. They followed the aroma directly to the backyard.

"Gentlemen, to what do I owe this pleasure and who the hell are you guys?" he said with a friendly lilt.

"Name is Kelly and this is Michael Davis and we just need to ask you a few questions," Jim replied, distracted by the atypical winter smell of someone actually outside cooking in the thirty degree chill.

"Can I offer you guys something to eat, a beer, or soft drink?" Mitchum asked in a jovial manner. Immediately, Kelly was confident that this relaxed working class guy was probably one they could cross off their list.

Michael jumped at the chance for a grilled brat and told Mitchum he would love to try the chef's specialty, but they would drink water, as they were on duty. Mitchum motioned them into the house through the sliding patio door and sat down with them.

After identifying himself and Michael as Philadelphia police officers, Kelly began. "We are investigating the shooting at the insurance convention in Center City several months ago. Our records show that you were in the area that day and crossed back into New Jersey slightly after the incident," Kelly stated, removing a pen and small spiral notepad from his pocket. "We just need to know where in Philly you were and what you were doing."

"That's an easy one, guys," he replied without missing a beat. "My oldest graduates high school this year and had an appointment at Temple University, hopes to go there in the fall. His car was in the shop, had to take mine. As a favor, he picked me up a duck at Sang Kee over on Ninth, so the time he got back probably coincided."

Kelly and Michael both spoke up; Michael yielded to his senior and Kelly thanked Mitchum for the information. It seemed to be another in a growing stack of dead ends.

Mitchum excused himself, grabbed a large plate and opened the patio door. He returned with a platter full of brats snuggled in hard rolls and three burgers, topped with sharp provolone from DiBruno's in South Philly.

The three savored their sandwiches and sipped their beverages, talking about the Eagles upcoming season; all were in agreement that *this was the year*. In reality, there never was a *year* as the city was still void of a super bowl title and the bragging rights that accompanied it.

They both thanked him for his hospitality and gourmet lunch, one of the perks of being a cop, and shook his hand before heading off to their second stop.

The next interview was nearby with a woman named Jaime Valle. She also resided in Cherry Hill and both men agreed it would probably be another wasted stop.

They followed the drone directions from the GPS and arrived at the condo twenty minutes later. They parked in a visitor spot and Michael lowered his chair from the middle door of the handicapped van. The unit was on the first floor, which was good because there were no elevators or easy access to the second level. When they arrived at the door, Kelly knocked three times as there was no doorbell button to push. Jaime, glued to the news of her late night activities and slightly buzzed from the Grey Goose martini she was so deft at concocting, barely heard the knock until it was repeated with a bit more intensity.

"Hang on; hang on, gimme a minute. Be right there," came a faint response that was barely audible to the pair.

She hopped off the couch. She was not expecting company but knew her friend Meg would show up unannounced at odd times. But, peering through the peephole, she didn't recognize the figure standing at her door.

"Can I help you?" she queried in an innocent yet assertive voice.

"Officers Kelly and Davis, ma'am. We are from the Philadelphia Police Department. May we speak to you for a moment?"

"Sure, okay. Give me minute to throw something on. Be right there," she said in a tone that had a slight hint of nervousness.

That meant little, as most people sound like that when the authorities show up unexpectedly.

Jaime instantly freaked out with images of being led away in handcuffs and charged with murder. She splashed some cold water on her face, mentally regrouped, and got rid of those ugly thoughts. She took a long, deep breath to regain her composure, strolled to the door and opened it. Her eyes were met first by Kelly, who stood holding out his credentials. She then shifted her gaze to Michael, who sat in his wheelchair, also holding his identification out for her to examine. Her eyes locked on his. There was no apparent reason for this new and uncontrollable reflex. Even more befuddling was that his eyes locked on hers simultaneously.

"I am Kelly and this is Davis. May we speak to you and ask some questions?"

"Sure, and this is in reference to?" Jaime said still with a morsel of nervousness in her response.

"We are just doing some follow up in regard to the shooting of the insurance people at the Constitution Center several months ago. We're checking on all the vehicles that crossed the Ben Franklin near, or close to, the time of the shootings. Is that okay?" he asked in a disarming tone.

"That's fine with me. Please come in. Would either of you care for something to eat or drink?"

Both declined as they were full from their last meal. The strangest thing was that Michael and Jaime had not broken their locked gazes ever since he entered. Jaime was perplexed by her actions, as they were a new experience. Michael was just plain mesmerized by her beauty and intensity, something he had not felt in a while and something that was totally unexpected. Since he had been back from the war and had lost a great deal of confidence, this feeling that was soaking into him was new. It was also uplifting to his being and his manhood.

Time seemed to freeze as Michael replayed some of his favorite dates and relationships before he sustained his crippling injuries. He superimposed Jaime's features into some of his past loves, but it was done automatically and not with any thought. He shook his head in an attempt to clear these thoughts and bring him back to the here and now. It worked.

Having more experience and training than Michael, Kelly took the lead during this informal interrogation.

"Miss Valle, we just need to ask you about your visit to the city the day of the shootings. It's more about filling out this report as to those who might have seen something and what they were doing," he stated nonchalantly.

"Like they do on *Law & Order*; I just love that show," she responded, trying to give herself a little time to construct her alibi.

"Yes, like *Law & Order*," Michael said, not wanting to be left out of the mix.

"Well, let's see," she began. "It was several months ago and I go into the city many times a month. Yeah, okay, I went to the Italian Market to get some pasta and cheeses over on Ninth Street. That was around ten or ten thirty. Then I jumped on Seventh toward the bridge. I wanted to get some dumplings and duck for lunch over at Sang Kee."

Michael watched her closely to study her body language, something that Treble had been schooling him on during his time in Philly. He noticed her hands clasped, a possible sign of trying to hide something or to sound convincing, which she seemed to be.

Kelly jotted some notes down on her activities and then looked up, asking his next question.

"And after you left the restaurant? Was it before or after the shootings took place? And which street did you take to the bridge entrance?" His questions were in rapid succession, wanting to see just how quickly and confidently she responded.

"Okay. I left Sang Kee and made a right turn on Vine and took that to Sixth and turned onto the bridge. I don't know if it was before or after the shootings. There was only the usual traffic getting onto the bridge."

Jaime was certain that she was convincing, but her body language was telling Michael that she was either nervous or lying. He would discuss that in the car after they left.

"Got it," said Kelly. "But I will take you up on a glass of ice water, please," he finished.

As she headed to the kitchen with Cosmo, thinking it was food time, right behind her, Michael nodded at Kelly. Kelly got up and did a cursory inspection of the condo. He glanced at a group of photos, struck by one in particular. She was surrounded by a group of men, maybe family, all dressed in camouflage, indicating she was a hunter. It wasn't a rocket science conclusion because two dead bucks lay at their feet. He scribbled some more notes down. Maybe it was significant or maybe not, but their suspect list was thin and the case was growing colder by the day. A trophy also caught his attention, awarding first place in a target competition from over one hundred yards. Hearing Jaime shutting off the faucet, Kelly hurried back to his original position. He now had a possible lead and Jaime, the possible "person of interest," was clueless.

"Thanks for the water," Kelly said, as he sipped it until it was finished. "And thank you for your cooperation. We will get back to you if we have any further questions."

Michael, still in awe like a sixteen-year-old with a high testosterone level, resumed his fixation. As Kelly beckoned Michael to go, he told him to go on ahead as he wanted to speak to Jaime in private. Kelly obliged, pretty sure he knew what his questions were in reference to.

When the front door closed, Michael began.

"This is totally not me and I might even be breaking procedure. Would I be out of line to see if you would have dinner or lunch with me in the near future?"

She was not surprised by his request and her mind raced. Should she get involved, on any level, with someone investigating her? Or could she turn that into an advantage: playing Little Ms. Innocent and win him over?

"Let me give you my number. My husband recently passed away and you will be the first, well, the first date I will be on since then." Her tone combined sensitivity, enthusiasm and caution all in that one answer. She handed him her cell number. He smiled as he accepted the paper, thanking her and saying he would be in touch soon. He was also impressed that his handicap was not a factor and that she never asked how he ended up in that position. That impressed him even more.

Michael reached the van and rolled onto the lift that propelled him into the back seating area.

"Yo, stud muffin. What was that all about?"

"So where to next, Officer Kelly?" Michael responded, obviously avoiding the question.

"Back downtown, as I think we need to do a little bit of research on your new girlfriend."

They drove the rest of the way in silence. Both knew, although nothing was definite, that they had a lead they could dig their teeth into.

When they arrived, they rode the elevator up to the third floor and met at Kelly's desk. Michael had called Treble, who said he would be in after his lunch with Sarah. Sarah Dubbin had been one of the decoys that had helped capture Bruce Titell, the Internet stalker and killer who had terrorized the city last year. Since Treble would be in Philly for a while longer, he took an aggressive approach on the quest for Dubbin. She was younger, smart and sexy as hell. She was not only a challenge for Treble, but also a goddess.

Kelly and Michael worked independently and would compare notes when they had gathered all the background information they could. When Treble finally would arrive, Michael would fill him in on the interview and the small habits and inflections Jaime had expressed. Kelly began by checking on any warrants or priors that Jaime might have on record. Michael was running computer checks and hacking into her computer. He was using a trick that Geek had taught him to circumvent the hard drive, thus eliminating any evidence of his searches. After all, they did not have a warrant.

Kelly's search produced very little. She had a speeding ticket last year, but that was it. He found her marriage records and was able to trace her past history under her maiden name. He learned she grew up in Salem County, New Jersey, probably the most rural of all in the state. She had three brothers, which explained the other males in the hunting photo. He also learned that she had been married and that her husband, Jeffery, had passed away less than a year ago. He was only thirty-one years old. He began a search on Jeff.

Michael began checking the websites on Jaime's computer. There were the usual shopping sites where she bought clothes. She purchased her books on Amazon, some various things on Overstock, and even had a Facebook page. She had also purchased some ammunition and hunting paraphernalia from Cabelas. Interesting, he thought. He then did a Google search to see if there might be anything pertinent.

"Yo, Kelly, check this puppy out," he called with obvious enthusiasm.

"Hold on kid, I'm coming."

Kelly walked over, placing his hand on the handle of the wheelchair and gazed at the screen. There was a picture of a younger Jaime. She was holding a trophy and ribbon for placing first in a shooting competition. Searching further, they learned that she was actually very well-known and recognized as a damn good markswoman. They looked at each other and knew what the other was thinking: that this woman needed some more looking into.

Just then, Treble entered the room with a shitfaced grin that stretched from ear to ear. There was no reason to ask where he had been and what he had done. His facial expressions spoke volumes.

"Hey, you guys, have you two been behaving or what?" he said in a jovial manner.

The three men punched fists with each other, as this was the new trend replacing high fives.

The pair briefed Treble on the recent interview with Jaime, filling him in on both the conversation and her behavioral patterns. Treble was a *profiler extraordinaire;* pulling up a chair, he listened intently, asked some questions and took notes. He then perused the screen, wanting to see both her background and how she appeared in the photos. The pair anxiously awaited his first impressions, still believing they were onto something.

"Okay. My guttural instincts are as follows: we have a woman who is competitive, adept at shooting and alone. We need to find out about her husband and how he died. We should gather more info and try to get a warrant for her computer and residence, as there might be some documents, weapons or something that will either clear her or nail her. The lead is promising, but we need more info. Check up on some of her friends and her place of employment. But do it in a subtle way. Farther down the road, I will pay her a visit, which will help me get a better feel for who she is," Treble stated.

"You two did a good job. Within a short time we should have a better idea as to whether or not she may have been our shooter."

"Should we fill out a report and send it upstairs?" Michael asked, wanting to follow protocol.

"Fill out the standard report and we will run it by the brass at the weekly meeting. At least we have a qualified lead. And let's keep this quiet so that we can be thorough without anyone breathing down our necks."

Kelly and Michael returned to their computers. They were pumped up at the progress they had made as well as from the positive feedback from Treble. It was what investigative work was all about.

"Yo, I like the way you are approaching this and know how and why this might be tough. Enough said. Use that charm and get a date with her. It might even clear her, but you have to realize the implications if it doesn't. We need to solve this case and that's the numero uno priority."

"Gotcha," replied Michael in a non-committal tone.

He then asked to be excused, knowing what he had to do but, at the same time, not really wanting to do it.

He wheeled himself over to an unused room which had a desk and a phone. He pulled out his wallet and removed the slip of paper that contained her phone number. Closing the door behind him, he took out his cell phone rather than using the using the landline, just in case.

He first punched in the number to save it in his address book, he then redialed the number and waited for her to answer.

She picked up on the second ring.

"Jaime speaking," she said spritely.

"Jaime, hi, it's Michael, from the other day," he responded with a hint of nervousness in his voice.

"Hi Michael, this is an unexpected treat. It's so nice you called so soon. What's up?" Jaime replied in a way that added to Michael's uncertainty about his timing.

"To tell you the truth, I was really looking forward to calling. It's weird. I hate to admit it, but I got this good feeling from yesterday and I am not usually this forward with my emotions."

Jaime, sensing the need to reinforce his confidence, interrupted.

"Me, too, I got the same strange vibes, which is something that so not happens to me," she said, knowing her answer would add a bit of faith to his lack of confidence. She continued.

"I hope I passed your interview," Jaime said with a mixture of innocence and curiosity.

Michael thought carefully before answering, torn between his sworn duties and his newly found infatuation.

"It was just background stuff, ya know. That's how we eliminate and pare down our leads. You have nothing to worry about, unless of course you killed that guy." He was deliberate in the way he made that comment, making sure she would interpret it as a bad joke.

"Yup, I have committed all unsolved crimes in the Delaware Valley so, when we go out, don't forget the handcuffs and stuff," she replied, trying to be as casual as he had been.

But she gave him the signal that he was looking for. She said "when we go out" which meant she too was into it. He smiled. That smile was accompanied by a small lift in his pants.

"When is easy. How about Friday, unless one day's notice is cutting it close. And by the way, I will explain how I ended up in this chair, but I can assure you that everything else still functions." Getting carried away by the moment, he wished he could retract that overly suggestive comment.

"First of all, I am not too concerned about the chair and, secondly, if it didn't work before, maybe we can make it into a project so it starts to work again." She knew that innuendo would score big.

"Whoa. Let's continue this tomorrow as I don't want to get into any trouble here before we even meet up."

"Okay, Mr. Michael Davis. Who is picking who up, what time and where are we going?" Her voice was not only sexy but also captivating.

"I will get you at seven tomorrow and call right before I arrive. Since it's your turf, your pick the place and the only thing I don't like is Middle Eastern food."

"Deal, I will see you tomorrow then, and thanks for the call. So glad you did."

Michael hung up. He had a feeling that had been missing for years and he was so excited to get it back.

CHAPTER NINETEEN

Abby and Bryant slept well on the flight home, which was about the longest period of sleep they had since their Florida vacation began. They had thoroughly enjoyed their stay and Bryant immediately like Allie. Both women took full advantage of their escape from the cold weather and current news that engulfed Philadelphia. What could have been bad? Abby was able to catch up with a longtime friend, catch some rays and even have her own one night stand. Bryant was happy to escape the trial that had pitted her ex against his high level mob bosses. She felt kind of stupid that she had been oblivious to how deep his involvement had been. She wondered if it was denial or that the less she knew or thought the better. She ate well, had her own much needed fling and was happy that she was becoming closer to Abby. The fact that Abby had been partially responsible for her breakup with Gando made her mad at first, but now she was forgiving, knowing what kind of man she had fallen in love with.

"I think we both need a vacation from that vacation, "said Bryant, her eyes half open.

"Not to change subjects, but what do you think about maybe a move down to Florida? After all, there is nothing of real consequence holding us in this Neanderthal city. Is there?"

"It's definitely something to consider. We could start a business. The weather is better. Places to live are super cheap. It is so worth some serious consideration."

"It sounds to me that you just voted for the move by an overwhelming majority. I'm all for it," gushed Abby with a girlish enthusiasm. "Let's have some serious discussions and make some decisions as soon as we can. I am ready to boogie."

The plane touched down in a near perfect landing, followed by scattered applause from some rookie travelers. The two women stood from their seats, opened the overhead compartment for their carry-ons and exited the plane. They were in no great rush to arrive at baggage claim; baggage claim could garner a two hour wait on a bad night and, considering the current full moon, this could be one of those nights. Since it was Friday, they agreed to return to their respective residences and spend Saturday doing their post-vacation catch up on mail and calls. They agreed to meet for brunch on Sunday to discuss packing up and leaving the City of Brotherly Love in their rear view mirrors.

****

Gando was usually cool. He was generally unaffected in precarious situations and was always well aware of his surroundings. He had been shuffled around the past several weeks, mainly for his protection, but was now getting antsy. The trial was over and he had neither any control over nor a hint as to the outcome. Regardless, a deal was a deal and he would be entering witness protection in the very near future. During his time in seclusion, he had done some soul searching as to where he should reside. After much thought and several discreet phone calls, he decided to move to the Fort Lauderdale area. Several reasons led him to this decision.

For one, the area was warm, clean, and had more affordable housing, having yet to recover from the real estate depression. Gando never forfeited two of his well hidden stashes of cash that he had saved for the proverbial rainy day. One was located in a safe deposit box that he had procured along with one of his fake identities. The other was in good hands with his longtime friend, Jake Crello.

Jake had grown up three houses down from Gando during his elementary and high school years in Hoboken. They were inseparable. Jake was his right hand man during all the minor trouble they had gotten into in those years, like the time when they planted some dope in one

husband and she too was in the same position. Since she had never mentioned the circumstances of his passing, Michael made a mental note to look into it the following day. After all, he had to bring something back from his assigned duties as an investigator on this case.

On the short ride home, they listened to classic rock, which Jaime had mentioned she was quite fond of. They both were. When he pulled up to the development, Jaime spoke first.

"I had an awesome evening. To be honest, I was kind of expecting it, or at least hoping it would be an extension of our initial connection," she said enthusiastically as she watched Michael's face brighten.

"And I as well, could you tell?" he said, watching Jaime smile.

They leaned across the seats at the same time. No words were spoken as their lips were too busy with other priorities. Several minutes later they separated, wanting to stop and save any fireworks for a future encounter. Michael said his good night, adding he would call and hoped that they could do it again. Jaime quickly agreed. She got out, waved once and Michael waited till she was safely inside. He couldn't have been any happier or more excited as he drove out of her neighborhood.

CHAPTER TWENTY

The next morning, Michael sat in a conference room with Treble, Kelly and his brother. He recounted the evening's conversations with them, not wanting to miss any clues or diversions she might have offered. Michael was still new to this, and only experience would give him insight on how to listen for hidden meanings as well as read body language. According to Michael, it said a lot that she rarely crossed her arms and was fluid in her motions. It told Treble that she was comfortable with Michael and did not view him as a threat. This was a good thing. On their next date, Michael would be schooled in not only what to ask, but also how to ask it. This might reveal some different aspects of her personality. They also decided to put a loose tail on her for the next several weeks, just to learn her habits and friends.

The team was excited about this new lead but would continue their interviews with other folks whose license plates had been recorded that day to be as thorough as possible. Investigative work had taught them that things never appeared as they seemed. And even though the case had died down in the media, it still reared its head when space needed to be filled on a slow news day.

****

Gando paced. Today would be day two of deliberations and he would not be allowed to relocate until the trial was over. His newly appointed handler from the Witness Protection Program sat opposite him in the hotel lobby having breakfast.

Matt Pacone was a dark haired, well-seasoned professional, having never lost any individuals he entered into the program. He was pragmatic and analytical, graduating from Boston University with dual degrees in psychology and criminal justice. He had been an active agent with the FBI, but was recalled from the field following a severe gunshot wound during a sting operation. It slowed down his reaction time, but his mind was as sharp as ever.

"Julian, I have reviewed your request and itinerary and have several questions," he began in a non-emotional tone. "Go over with me who you are staying with and some background on your relationship, please."

Gando continued to slather butter on his whole wheat toast. He dipped it into his runny eggs and looked up.

"I thought we went through this," he began sounding slightly annoyed.

Pacone had his pen out, poised to check his notes and add any details that might have been omitted or could cause a problem. He always thought ahead, which is why his unblemished record still stood.

"It's an old buddy of mine, Jake Crello, and I trust him with my life. Gimme a break, you guys have checked him out ten times over. Am I right or am I right?"

Pacone ignored the sarcasm and waved him to continue.

"He lives outside of Lauderdale and owns some horses he races at the local tracks. He and I have also discussed opening a small Italian restaurant, ya know, with New York type of dishes that seems to have avoided the move to Florida. I've always wanted to do that and I can keep a low profile. I plan to bunk down with Jake until I can find a place to live and he agreed to do all the legwork in regard to a location for the place."

"And the capital you need for this venture?" Pacone asked curiously, one eyebrow rising up while the other stayed put.

"I am calling in a marker with Jake. I helped finance one of his past ventures and told him to keep it until a time might come when I needed it back. Now is the time."

That was a partial truth, as Gando still had a bounty of cash, some entrusted to Jake which was as good as being in the bank.

Gando ate in silence as Pacone scribbled notes into the margins of his neatly typed document. His mind wandered about his upcoming freedom, something he had sorely missed during this whole ordeal. He avoided replaying the events that led to his capture and the mistakes he had made that had landed him in this unnecessary situation. Just like in the old classic 1940's black and white movies, it was a "dame" that had gotten him in trouble. The main difference was he would not attempt to win Bryant's affections back or seek revenge against Abby for setting him up. He would move on and learn from his mistake.

As Pacone put down his pen and stretched, he noticed a pair of men dressed in similar leather coats over black hoodies which partially obscured their features. In a New York second, he rose and, grabbing Gando's shoulder, threw him under the table with almost superhuman force. He shouldered rolled onto the floor, pulling his gun as he watched for any indication of weapons. Two agents who worked with Pacone were sitting at the opposite side of the restaurant by the exit to the hotel, dressed inconspicuously in construction denims; they were just as quick. Unlike the movies, nothing was going in slow motion but rather was happening in what appeared to be fast-forward.

The man in the lead was now aware of the small legion of agents as he reached into his waistband. But he was unable to grab his semi-automatic machine pistol before three shots struck him almost simultaneously and he was propelled backwards. His associate had been able to pull his weapon but was met with the same fate. A quarter-sized cavity appeared in his forehead while two separate shots found their mark in his heart area, the blood spraying out in a fountain-like cascade.

In less than ten seconds and a dozen loud explosions, the two lay dead only several steps from the street entrance to the dining area. The smell of gunpowder and fresh blood wafted through the room. The half dozen diners were silent and the motion in the room seemed suspended in time.

"Is everyone all right?" Pacone yelled in an authoritative tone, as sound began to return to the room.

The two other agents confirmed they were and Gando slowly arose from beneath the table. His face was white, but he was void of emotions and any look of surprise. After all, the experience was not that new to him. The only bright side was that he was still alive.

The agents approached the amateur assassins, kicking their guns away, more out of training than necessity. One agent called in to report the incident while the other called in for medical transport. Pacone briskly escorted Gando out and back up to his room. In several minutes, reporters would arrive and the area would be the lead story on the noon TV news shows and future headline in the morning newspapers.

The Daily News did not disappoint as it penned another creative headline: **"Missing Breakfast Kills Two"**

CHAPTER TWENTY-ONE

The Daily News story was written in pure Philly-speak. The story was mixed with sarcasm, a touch of humor and a less than heaping teaspoon of the cold hard facts. It read as follows:

"A suburban chain hotel is not the typical high profile location for an assumed Organized Crime assassination. Sparks Steak House and the Melrose Diner are far more well known. But when it comes to revenge, there is no concern for location, location, location.

When two gunmen entered the small hotel lobby, covered with hoodies and armed with semi-automatic weapons, three well-trained federal agents were armed and ready. Both intruders were shot dead before they could even get off a shot. No identifications have yet to be made, as neither man was carrying any. Sources close to the Feds believe it might have been two hired Russian hit men, as both had tattoos which have been identified to Russian hit squads. Sources also told the Daily News that Gando had no beef with the men and the assumption is that they were hired by one or both of the men on trial as a payback for his testimony."

The story continued with a summary of the case that led up to its current state of jury deliberation. Pictures of the two men on trial as well as Gando framed the story.

The morning story might have been that one event they someday would look back upon as a turning point in their lives. As Bryant and Abby drank lunch time Cosmopolitans and picked on tasty appetizers at a trendy Center City eatery, they *knew*.

"I think that it's time, girlfriend," said Abby, as Bryant had a distant stare written on her face.

It wasn't that she still had feelings for Gando, but she didn't want to see him gunned down in public, either. There was nothing holding the two women from starting anew in a faraway place. They both were hardly working, both had substantial savings accounts and both were still young and attractive with an inkling of adventure and the unknown circulating through their personas.

Bryant's absent look began to disappear, replaced by a smile and mischievous expression that was foreign to her close friend. She sighed and then spoke.

"Okay, you are right. Let's figure out the when and where, put our houses on the market with our realtors and vanish," she said, grabbing Abby's hand with a solid expression of determination. There was also a rare moment of spontaneity that had been generally missing from Bryant's traits, but maybe it was now emerging after that one night stand in Florida.

****

It was a busy Friday during the final official week of winter; the first day of spring was quickly approaching. And if Punxsutawney Phil was correct, the crisp spring air would be helping the smooth transition from winter. Across the Delaware River in Hamilton, New Jersey, located near the state capitol of Trenton, Dr. Charles Bellnap was finishing up the final report on Kim Carole. Two state detectives were joined by the now roving criminalist, Dieter Treble, who had asked to be contacted because of the woman's occupation. His curiosity and experience guided him to this meeting. She had worked in the insurance industry, and two assassinations in that short a time got his attention. And besides, maybe he could add another investigation to the one growing colder by the minute in Philadelphia. The office in Hamilton has the distinction of being one of the four labs nationwide with an agreement with the FBI to analyze evidence for Mitochondrial DNA. That type of DNA testing examines the smallest chromosomes and is used to help determine victims' identities. In this case, however, the body had been identified and that specific testing was not needed.

year all the way up to six. Minutes later, the pair was found guilty of bookmaking.

Out of the fifteen charges, the pair was found guilty on only two charges. After the weekend, the trial would resume with arguments regarding the sentencing. They could receive anywhere from two to ten years in jail. Regardless of that outcome, appeals would follow and Judge Judy would have to decide if the two would be set free during the appeals or remanded into the Pennsylvania prison system. In either case, the media would have a field day, or rather field weekend, speculating on the final outcome and ruling.

The OCTF team had decided to meet back at the Roundhouse after the verdict, regardless of the outcome. It was a small victory but how small would not be known until the following week.

Bracci and Mancini were taken out of the courtroom. Their smiles had somewhat faded but the lilt in their steps hardly reflected their disappointment in beating nearly all of the charges that had been levied against them. Their respective sons were given several minutes with them, guards being present and both still in handcuffs. What was said during those several minutes was only privy to those involved, but did all who witnessed the meeting think that their words were anything but evil?

****

All the members of the OCTF, including Treble and Finnegan, were back at the Round House. Disappointment in their expressions was obvious but there were no signs of defeat. They regrouped in Conference Room B, which had now become what they called the "war room." They maintained a positive attitude, confident that Judge Judy would be generous with their sentences. That was her reputation.

After some discussions, reactions and congratulations, the gathering broke up. Stephen, Kelly, Geek and Treble all remained, along with several task force members who were the most trusted and experienced. They needed to discuss the prior events that took place in Trenton. Before the meeting, Treble had asked Michael if he were seeing Jaime again and he replied they had a date tomorrow night. He cautioned him to be careful and in the same breath handed him an assignment in an envelope marked PRIORITY. This was done for two reasons. First, Michael was one of the best computer guys they had. This new case involved several dubious bank transactions and transcripts regarding transfers by questionable Middle Eastern sympathizers. They worked out of Philadelphia, which made it fall into the OCTF jurisdictional realm of investigations.

The second reason was to divert Michael away from the case involving Jaime. In the event that his feelings might influence his responsibilities, he would be more of a problem than a solution to the ongoing investigation. His brother had signed off on it, wanting to protect his younger brother from doing anything he might regret so early in his new career. Michael was told it was a priority and to get started as soon as he left the room. Treble assured him that he would be kept abreast of Jaime's involvement, if any, in the current case.

The remaining group sat and placed some one dollar bets on the outcome of the sentence. Judge Putnam was known for being tough yet fair, causing them to assume she would lean toward a maximum sentence. Treble cleared his throat, the universal sign that he wanted the floor and the participants to give him their undivided attention. They did.

Before he began, Treble mentioned why he had siphoned Michael off the case. The rest of the group agreed with the idea and promised to keep him on a need-to-know basis in order not to compromise their progress.

"Okay, you guys," he began with a poor attempt at Philly slang.

"I want to fill you in on some of the forensics that was discovered on the Carole murder. The bullet recovered was a match to the ones used at our Constitution Center crime scene. The Jersey State Police are looking into the woman's background and are checking her acquaintances. And we are also looking into Ms. Jaime Valle: her past and her husband's. My contacts in the bureau traced a very interesting and incriminating factor. Jeff Valle had passed away in the hospital while awaiting a procedure. His insurance claim had been approved at first, then denied and appealed. By the time it was re-approved, he had expired. The senselessness and preventability of his death might have set Jaime off. It's a theory, but a good one. Couple this with the fact that she is a more than competent shot with a rifle. Add in the fact that she was in the city the day of the attacks and we now have a person of extreme interest."

Treble looked up at the expressions of these seasoned investigators and knew they were on the same page with him.

"The fact is that we all know that one plus one plus one does not always equal three. It's promising but there is one variable that really throws me," said Davis.

"And that is?" Treble asked with a hint of what was to follow.

"We have never heard of, let alone met, a female sniper serial killer. But then again...." His voice trailed off. His experience had taught him that the old cliché "anything is possible" was especially true when dealing with criminal behavior.

Davis added that they would seek search warrants for Jaime's condo and her husband's medical records and run a full background search of her whole life before going any further. Any grand jury hearings or questioning were still in the future. They would continue with the investigation, just in the event that a secondary promising suspect were to emerge. They also discussed the need for secrecy with Michael. As long as he had a non-threatening rapport with the suspect, she might feel more at ease with her perceived anonymity in the killings.

✳✳✳✳✳✳✳✳✳✳✳✳✳✳✳✳✳✳✳✳✳✳✳✳

In the computer room, Michael was diligently working on the new case that he was given. He had gotten through several dozen pages, checking bank records, routing numbers and transfers made by the suspects. It was tedious but necessary. He was deeply emerged. But two hours into his research, a giant freight train of a thought entered the right side of his brain. He knew that computer research was one of his areas of expertise, but he couldn't help but wonder if he was being eased out of the current investigation due to his involvement with Jaime. He picked up his cell to call his brother; he placed it down on the desk almost as quickly. He knew that Stephen would never compromise an investigation and he would never be able to pry information out of him. Truth serum and rubber hoses were not viable options. He also knew that calling Jaime was not an option. For one thing, he had no real information, only some suspicions. And, second, he did not want to alarm her, possibly risking an end to his date for tomorrow evening.

He did the only thing he could, something he had trained himself to do during and after his war time experiences: he blocked any relative thoughts of what to do out of his mind and immersed himself back into his new assignment.

CHAPTER TWENTY-THREE

The smoke gray skies that had hung over the city of Philadelphia for the past several days now gave way to a cloudless, bright blue background as the first day of Spring made its appearance. The day held meaning to Julian Gando, as this was to be his first day of the freedom he had missed during the long winter months. He would board a plane this morning and arrive in Florida by tomorrow. His flights would be indirect, just in case he was being followed. He would be accompanied by several agents and loosely tailed by a half dozen more. It was a necessary precaution in lieu of the recent failed assassination.

He would fly on three different carriers into three different cities. He would fly from Philadelphia to Atlanta, then from Atlanta to Houston, and finally from Houston to Tampa. This third flight would be on a small government aircraft and would land in a private government airfield. No witness had ever been followed or discovered during the relocation process.

"We have gone over all instructions, so please adhere to them to the letter," Pacone said in his ever-present monotone.

"Just as you wish, Matt," Gando responded. "After all, I do owe my life to you and the truth is you have been a standup guy."

Pacone nodded and ushered him into the car on the way to Philadelphia International Airport. They both hoped it would be an uneventful trip.

****

On that same spring morning, Jaime made the trip down route 295 to Jeffery's gravesite. It was a once-a-month short journey and it helped with her grieving process. She placed a colorful wreath of flowers upon the grave in a gentle manner.

Rather than speak to Jeffery verbally, her mind projected thoughts to him as if he could comprehend them, as she hoped he would. An inkling of guilt had come over her regarding the fact that she had enjoyed Michael's companionship on their first date, just as she had Jeffery's. Both first dates were held over dinner, were lighthearted, with no pressure felt by either party. Both warranted a second date as each of the men came off as gentle and well mannered. They also made her laugh. And feel comfortable, like she was the only woman alive.

It wasn't that she was looking for approval from her deceased husband, but rather she was testing her own integrity and guilt, and she discovered on the latter there was none. A small smile turned upward on her lips as she remembered how Jeff had always told her to "go with the flow," an old mantra from the seventies. Being a throwback to that era, she always did. And she would continue to regarding her unknown journey with Michael. She turned back to her car, feeling the uplift in her spirits that came after visiting her late husband's gravesite. It was a new day and a new season.

When she returned to the car she moved the rear view mirror to check her make-up. She dabbed a tissue on some of the dark lines caused by her mascara. When satisfied she was back together, she left the cemetery. She dialed her friend, Meg, to see if their tentative breakfast at Ponzios, a Cherry Hill New Jersey old school diner, was still on. They would meet at ten thirty in the hopes of avoiding the crowd for the morning breakfast special.

Meg was already seated by the window and waved in her patented, animated high speed motions. Jaime nodded, acknowledging she had seen her, and entered the eatery. Pushing through a crowd of Botox-laden faces and octogenarians in white loafers, she ignored the stares and headed toward Meg's booth at the window.

"Let's eat, I am so starved," Meg said in the semi-desperate voice which was one of her trademarks.

it did bring him back to the present. It told him that he was thinking too much and he needed to get back to the moment, and this particular moment was directed toward dinner, drinks and the passion that would follow.

That evening, Ashley made all of her lover's thoughts turn from work to pleasure, from worry to confidence, and, most importantly, from passivity to passion.

They spent the evening as if it were their first time together as well as their last. Their usual verbal banter was replaced by carnal expressions of pleasure. Their habitual unselfish activities were replaced by unrehearsed spontaneity. And their pleasures brought them to new and uncharted territories.

CHAPTER TWENTY-FOUR

Marco Bracci was awakened by three short rings of the phone that rested on the nightstand. Never once did any one of the Four Seasons hotels miss a wakeup call. While awaiting sentencing, his father had asked that he visit on Saturday to discuss some business that needed to be addressed. When he was in federal prison, all visits would probably be recorded and analyzed. At the detention center, this would not be the case.

Marco was feeling decadent. He called room service and ordered Eggs Benedict, two Bloody Mary's and a small serving of fruit to offset the calorie-laden breakfast. He showered, shaved and planned his day's activities. His emotions ran amok. The father who had mentored him would be serving some time, leaving a void in both the business and his close knit family. Conversely, he would now be the man in charge, a thought that elevated his ego and thirst for power. He had been well schooled in regard to the structure and hierarchy of his father's successful business. In some sort of convoluted way, he loved and respected his father, but in a selfish way that was more self-gratifying, he lusted for control, power and money.

He finished his breakfast. Marco was proud that he had avoided any type of prosecution so far in his budding career. He then began to dress and ready himself to meet with his soon-to-be-incarcerated father. In all the years that the elder Bracci had escaped any type of arrest, let alone a conviction, it was always in the back of Marco's mindset: the day had come, the reality had set in and now he had to step up to the plate.

Marco rode the elevator to the lobby where the one of the alert employees approached him.

"Anything I can help you with, Mr. Bracci?"

The fact he was called *mister* and that he had been remembered brought a smile to his face. After all, the Four Seasons was at the top of the hotel food chain.

"Yes, Raymond," he replied, glancing at the name tag that adorned the gold colored uniform. "A taxi is needed," he continued, with a bit of condescending pleasure in his tone.

Raymond blew the loud whistle as the next cab in line pulled up to the entrance. Before Marco entered the cab, he shoved a twenty dollar bill into Raymond's open hand. His immediate smile and gratitude stroked Marco's ego. He knew he made that guy's day.

The short ride up to where his father was being held gave Marco a brief snapshot of Philadelphia. His impressions were that of a miniature New York and he was unable to see the reason that his father had wanted to add it to his portfolio. But then again, that was why his father had been so successful. He was able to spot and seize a business opportunity and make it profitable.

His cab pulled up to its destination. He paid his fare with another generous tip, and headed toward the entrance. He opened the door to a metal detector with signs requesting that all items be emptied from one's pockets. He obliged and went through the designated passage. Clearing with no bells or alarms, he returned the items to his pockets and continued. He approached the information desk and, after a brief conversation, was directed to the right location.

Upon entering the visitor area, he handed the requisite card to the uniformed officer and was directed to a seat. He waited for several minutes before a guard brought his father out to the seat opposite him. It was separated by a plastic divider that ran up to the ceiling. A round cutout sat at face level to allow conversation.

Salvatore was a proud man and there were no signs of stress or concern etched upon any of his rugged features. His steel brown eyes sent a dictum of authority into Marco. He began to speak, but not before he glanced around for eavesdroppers.

into the music. He would deal with the situation when they had several cocktails and were settled in.

They arrived almost simultaneously at the valet. Michael had his chair out the driver's side door and was exiting his car. He learned to flash his badge, giving him a bit of special consideration; a disabled cop in a wheelchair grabbed people's attention. He waited by the entrance for Jaime to exit her car and she leaned over and kissed him gently on the lips.

"Were you following me, detective? "She asked jokingly.

"No need for that, as I placed a tracking device on your car," he replied in a similar fashion.

They both laughed as the doorman held the large glass door open for their passage. Michael gave the doorman a five, not as much to impress Jaime but rather in the spirit of the special night he was hoping for. They were led through the crowded bar area and back to a corner table. Through careful planning, their table was situated next to the two lucky agents who would dine on steak and wedge salads.

The pair ordered drinks, Jaime a Cosmo and Michael a dry martini with blue cheese stuffed olives. After the distinctive sounds of their glasses toasting the night, Michael began the conversation.

"Thank you so much for the second chance you have given me, I…"

Jaime interrupted, her eyes meeting his.

"What is this second chance crap," she said in a blunt manner. "The facts are we enjoy each other's company, no one forced me into this and I would like getting to know you better. Hope I am not being too forward," she ended. The expression on Michael's face indicated that she had said exactly the right thing.

The waiter brought the menus and went into his pre-rehearsed rant regarding the specials of the day. They stared at the menu, deciding to share a spinach salad and side of potatoes. Michael opted for the porterhouse while Jaime chose the lobster tail. She knew that men liked a woman's boldness when they ordered one of the most expensive items on the menu.

As the courses came, the conversation eased into various subjects. Whenever Michael broached the subject of the investigation, Jaime deflected it into an unrelated story or anecdote. Michael noted she was adept at interrogation, causing him to wonder if she had been there before.

The agents seated in near proximity wondered why Michael had been pussyfooting around the heart of the matter. They had been in on the original meeting when the basic outline of what to do had been created. And although everyone liked "the new kid on the block," they were experiencing a growing suspicion regarding where his loyalties lay. Back at the Roundhouse, where the conversation was being heard in real time, the same thoughts crossed their minds too.

Stehpen was becoming a bit impatient.

"Damn it, Michael, follow the freakin script we gave you. Get back on track," he said with condemnation, as if his brother could somehow hear his instructions.

"Easy, boss," said Kelly, having seen Davis fly off the handle on previous occasions when plans were not adhered to. He did tend to be a bit of a control freak at times, rarely trusting anyone to be able to carry out an assignment as well as he could.

The waiter came out on cue as the bus person was exiting with the cleared dinner plates. He handed them the dessert menu along with a short verbal description of several specials. They had already decided. Jaime took the lead and ordered two Irish coffees and a crème brûlée with two spoons.

Before Jaime spoke, she reached her hand across the table and rubbed one of her fingers over the knuckles of Michael's clenched fist which lay in front of him. Michael smiled, taking it as a good sign.

"I am having such a nice and comfortable evening, Mr. Michael Davis," she said in a soft voice.

Michael was speechless for a second and then, looking up into her eyes, told her that this was the best night he had experienced since his return back home. He took her finger in his hand, pulled it to his mouth and kissed it softly. Then, as if reading his mind, she suggested that they go back to her place for one last nightcap. She added that Cosmo and Oscar would likely be hungry for their dinner. He accepted. Fortunately, the pair didn't notice the men at the neighboring table; if they had, they would have seen one expressing an exaggerated eye roll and the other burying his forehead in his open hands. They were so glad to be here rather than back at headquarters where all hell was probably breaking loose. They had worked with the elder Davis on several occasions and knew what he was thinking and saying.

When the check arrived, Jaime insisted on dividing it but Michael would not hear of it. He peeled a pair of hundreds off his roll of bills and nodded, indicating it was time to go. Her offer was sincere but also cautious at the same time. What if Michael's house was bugged or someone was in the next room? Her place was safer.

They both left the restaurant, valet tickets and a tip in hand, and waited for their cars. She bent over him and gave him a kiss, thanking him for the fun and unexpected evening. The kiss was in between one of friendship and one of passion, but as she straightened up, she noticed the small tent in his pants indicating that he interpreted it as the latter.

The return trip home took less than half an hour. Jaime felt no pangs of guilt in her offer to Michael in regard to her late husband. She was concerned a bit, however, that her original agenda of keeping him close so she could learn about the investigation was now being challenged by a physical and emerging emotional attraction. During the ride home, she did the female thing: she analyzed her feelings and the possible outcomes that might follow.

Michael had thoughts on a different level, as most males would have. He ran a replay of the evening's conversations, body language and how things were said. Again, as most males do, all of his interpretations led him to the conclusion that he made an awesome impression and would reap the benefits of his emotional and physical desires.

They arrived at the condo and parked adjacent to each other. Michael did his car exit routine slightly faster than normal. Jaime was surprised to see him right behind her. She inserted the key, reached around to flip on the lights and Michael followed. Eight legs rushed toward her, complete with the expression of love and hunger to see their master had arrived. Cosmo even checked Michael out as his tail slowed momentarily, and then jumped up on his chair to offer a lick or two of approval.

She told Michael to make himself at home while she fed the kids. When she returned, he was on the couch looking quite at home.

"I hope you're not so quick in everything you do," she commented, noticing that Michael picked up on her not so subtle innuendo.

His quick reply was sharp and witty.

"Not at all, it's like dinner; the quicker you finish the main course, the longer you can savor the dessert."

The answer produced a warm and sincere smile from Jaime, one that Michael had yet to see in her repertoire. She placed two glasses of a clear liquid in front of them, mentioning that it was this new peach vodka she had gotten as a gift. If she had poured a glass of swill, it would have been just as inviting. He was in a place where he felt he belonged.

Jaime joined him on the couch, raising her glass to toast the wonderful dinner and company which she had just been treated to. The non-verbal gaze both confirmed her words and began what was to be a night void of verbal musings and full of silent pleasures.

CHAPTER TWENTY-FIVE

Crello bounced back from one leg to another, his nervous energy making him look like someone who had already consumed two dozen cups of coffee. Right on time, the expected black Expedition with tinted windows made its way up his circular driveway. Halfway down the block, a similar vehicle also stopped. It was the signal that Gando had arrived.

Two guys in obvious tourist garb exited the vehicle from the two rear doors. Next out was Gando who, upon seeing Crello, approached with open arms and a broad shit eating smile.

They were silent as they hugged for several seconds. As if their motions had been choreographed, they separated from their embrace and stepped backwards to examine each other.

"It's great to have you home, Julian. Wow. You look freakin dynamite," Crello said.

"Fuckn' A, Jake."

Gando was speechless as he stood staring at his old friend, his head shaking from side to side. Even the agents smiled, indicating they too probably knew what it was like to be reunited with a close buddy from the past.

"Why don't yous guys come in and have a drink. Ya probably need one after hanging out with this slug for the whole trip."

The agents thanked him for his hospitality but said they would take a rain check, mentioning that over the next several weeks, they would be stopping by to make sure all was safe. They did help carry in Gando's luggage and shook hands before parting. Gando thanked them with a heartfelt sincerity.

The pair went inside to have a drink and do some catching up. The two were separated by exactly one month in age and both had aged while retaining a good deal of their boyish features. Gando clearly retained more of his hair color and density, but Crello won in the areas of overall physique and well-tanned skinned. Crello excused himself and returned with two cocktails. The highball glasses were generously filled with 7 & 7's, their teenage drink of choice. The banged the glasses together and took long sips, evoking memories of the past.

The pair had stayed in contact sporadically since the old days, but had only gotten together once, at an old friend's funeral in Jersey. They spoke on occasion but the fact of the matter was they both knew that they could pick up their friendship at any time. This was now the time.

Crello had been briefly married in his thirties, but, after a year, he learned that he was better off single. Gando had not been able to attend the wedding, but did receive a check for five hundred dollars, the amount paid to the guy who remained single the longest. In return, he sent a thousand dollar gift to the newlyweds.

After Julian unpacked and took a shower, he was feeling hungry, the pair left for brunch. Gando expressed a craving for some stone crabs and Crello promptly agreed, also being a fan of the seasonal Florida staple. They hopped into Jake's vehicle and drove down the road to his local spot. Crello made a not-so-subtle comment that the same car that had been parked up the street from his house was loosely following them. Gando mentioned he didn't mind. They were there for his benefit and in the near future he would be on his own.

They parked, strolled inside and were granted their requested dockside table. The free-flowing ocean represented freedom to Julien, something he had been deprived of during his long ordeal. For the next two hours they reminisced about the good old days and filled in the blanks over the time that had transpired up until now. Gando gave abbreviated versions of his history, not wanting Crello to feel any empathy or concern over his past illegal activities. Crello was a bit more open, offering vivid details as any high school history book might. They laughed, soaked up the new information and bonded as their old friendship was rekindled. Gando even felt good that time had healed his history with Bryant and looked forward to the unknown future ahead of him.

✳✳✳✳✳✳✳✳✳✳✳✳✳✳✳✳✳✳✳✳✳✳

Many hundred miles up the northern seaboard, the City of Brotherly Love was not holding true to its name. Michael and Stephen sat across from each other at a local Philadelphia diner, tucked away in the back adjacent to the restrooms. It was not a frequently requested table.

The waitress came by with coffee, which both accepted, but the mood at the table was far from friendly. She took their order and, almost before she turned toward the kitchen, Michael began his controlled tirade.

"Let me see if I have this right, little brother." His tone was condescending and nasty.

"Let's turn back the clock. You get back from overseas, lead an irresponsible existence and then decide you want to do something constructive. Okay then. You work for the force, a high profile case and help to solve it. You then get fired up about a career, join the team and make police work a priority. Hello!!! Now you are involved in another high profile case, are assigned to gain the trust of our number one person of interest and then? Fill in the blanks, little brother."

Michael didn't even look up as his brother ripped him a new one. He knew what he was saying was right, but his emotional and physical needs surpassed his duties, both as an officer and as a sibling. Plain and simple, he knew he fucked up. Implacably, Stephen continued.

"Remember when you were in the Gulf? All the guys in your outfit depended on you. You watched each other's' backs and you were a team. Same holds true back here on American soil, bro."

Stephen felt bad about the oral beating he had given to Michael, but he would have done the same with any of those under his command who had flat out ignored their responsibilities. Michael, eyes red and moist, wore a look on his face somewhere between guilt and worthlessness. He felt his brother had been a bit over the top but also knew it was his way of making a point. After a deafening silence, his head rose up slowly as he readied a response.

"I have no excuses; I failed you and the whole team who had all been depending on me. It is obvious that neither an apology nor an excuse can express how badly I messed up. Everything you said is right and I am willing to face up to whatever actions you deem necessary. But I would also like to add that if I could replay the whole scenario, I would." His voice now projected a tone of sincere regret. He added that he was prepared to accept like a man whatever was doled out.

Stephen's thoughts flashed back to their youth, recalling a handful of events in which his younger brother had acted more on impulse than on intelligence. No one is immune to lapses of common sense or virtue, he thought to himself. He had even lashed out at Kelly on several occasions. Hell, even once on his lover, Ashley. But his lectures were not meant to be as much critical as they were to be a lesson, a lesson not to make the same error twice.

With a look that had turned from anger to compassion, he addressed Michael again.

"I know that you are the last person I have to explain myself to. Michael, I love you and care for you. I don't want to see you lose sight of the big picture, or of our common goals. We have been entrusted not only to protect our citizens but also to bring justice to those who have wronged them. You are more than capable of both of these directives and the next time shit like this happens, you will act in the right way."

Before he could speak, Stephen added one last addendum to his brief soliloquy.

"Obviously, you are officially off this case. I am relegating you some less pressing cases that need someone with your computer skills to gain more insight. Give this woman a rest, at least until we can either indict or clear her. Then and only then can you renew this budding romance," Stephen ended as he painstakingly avoided any traces of sarcasm and disapproval.

CHAPTER TWENTY-EIGHT

Gando was getting pretty used to his new life style. The condo he had selected turned out to be a good choice. He had met some people from the east coast who had moved down permanently, doubtfully for the same reason that he relocated here. He had taken on a new persona, complete with a more low key profile.

He had even taken Pacone's advice and had some minor plastic surgery done. He was also pushed into it by Crello.

A week after his arrival in Florida, Gando went to see a plastic surgeon about a rhytidectomy, which is more commonly known as a facelift. The procedure involved making several incisions in the areas of his forehead and chin. Excess fat was removed and the skin was re-draped to tighten his face and, ultimately, alter his appearance. It made a noticeable change, which was the intended result. He even paid in cash and was given a discount; only in America.

He also visited one of those hair restoration places that dominate the three-in-the-morning infomercial time slots, adding more hair to the emerging thinning in the center of his scalp. He also changed the color to a light brown, making him look less like himself as well as less Italian.

At first when he shaved in the morning, he would wonder who was looking back at him, but he grew more accustomed to his face and the ten years it took off his appearance. Crello was actually a bit jealous and always kidded him about it, and the thirty-one year old woman who lived in the neighboring building took special interest in it. They screwed several times a week.

During the past three months, he and Crello rekindled the buddy-buddy relationship they had formed back in their formative years. They spent time at Gulfstream Park, betting the ponies and hanging out with the usual derelicts that frequent betting establishments. They drank and gambled at the Seminole Hard Rock Hotel and Casino, establishing credit lines and getting comp meals for their above average play.

On a more productive level, they had found a new mall going up and quickly reserved a twenty-four hundred square foot empty store that they would convert into Johnny's Bistro, using the name of their favorite Italian restaurant during their time in Jersey. They shopped for repossessed restaurant equipment for sale, knowing that only one in five restaurants ever succeeds. They brainstormed about all the little touches they could add in order to make their customers feel like they were back in New York or New Jersey. They would have a takeout counter by the entrance, hanging fresh salami, sharp provolone, and cloves of garlic, giving it the feel and smell of a Little Italy market. They nixed the idea of a Marlon Brando "Godfather" cut out by the doorway; there is a limit to tackiness.

For Crello it was a new business adventure and challenge. He had made almost everything he touched turn to gold during his past years; Gando's return on investment was living proof. For Gando it was a combination of several things. For one, it had been quite some time since he had walked the straight and narrow. Secondly, owning a restaurant seems to be a dream that many home cooks and foodies seem to chase after. But the most important reason was the challenge, that of building something from the ground up. To take an idea, a concept, to roll the dice, give it your all and hopefully be successful all on one's own volition.

They decided that each phase needed to be agreed upon by the partnership. They interviewed contractors, went over all design ideas, the layout and, finally, the menu and the clientele they wished to attract. At times it was tedious, but as their plans went from paper to actual reality, they found their energy level and enthusiasm growing as each project took shape. It would be a matter of a month or two before the doors opened and their dreams would become reality; hopefully a profitable one. They would open right around Memorial Day, in time for the mass exodus of snowbirds from the thawing northeast.

"Do you remember what you purchased?"

"I think some cheeses from DiBruno's, some sausages, some pasta and some veggies from the street."

"And you paid how, cash or credit?" Treble asked.

"Maybe some of each; it was so long ago I don't remember."

Davis wrote that down in his small spiral pocket-sized notepad. It was impractical but it was the same type that Peter Falk used when he portrayed Colombo.

The next line of questioning was initiated by Davis. It centered on her gun collection. He needed to know where she had bought them, her shooting history and her trophies. As she answered his questions, they observed less tension in her voice and her body seemed to ease. Her passion for guns and shooting was transparent.

Treble abruptly interrupted.

"Is it possible you could show us your weapons? It will save us the trouble of getting a warrant, unless you prefer us to take that route."

"No, not at all," she confidently replied.

She arose and headed for the hall closet. A tall gun safe was visible, seeming to meet all legal requirements as far as storing a weapon was concerned. She removed a key from the top shelf, removed the rifle and handed it to Davis for closer inspection. He recognized immediately that it was not the same make or caliber used in the shootings. As any good investigator knows, always ask questions that you have the answer to. Davis and the team had pulled her gun registrations out well before hand and he knew she was hiding the rifle in question. It would be one more item to add to the impending search warrant. Also included on the warrant would be credit card receipts for the day in question as well as correspondence with her deceased husband and the health care physicians and any insurance company communications. Phone records too would be scrutinized.

Treble concluded the questioning along a more philosophical avenue.

"Miss Valle, if I may say, I don't know a lot of women into hunting. Noticing you have pets you are an obvious animal lover. Why do you hunt?"

The question was not totally unexpected as she had been asked that before. Assuming a rigid posture, she answered.

"Well, detective, as you know I have brothers, and men are competitive. I got into hunting not only as a way of bonding with them, but also to compete with them." Treble also now leaned closer.

"So killing is okay with you along those particular lines. How do you feel about people who kill others? I mean if there is a justification. Something like jealousy, hatred, or say even revenge."

The word revenge was said slowly and deliberately emphasized to get a non-verbal response. He got the one he was expecting. He got the one of someone who just might kill for a justified or perceived reason.

Treble motioned with his eyes to Davis that he was ready. They both arose and offered to shake her hand as they thanked her for the time. Not once was the subject of Michael Davis broached by either of the two who were at the spectrum of relationships with him. They exited just as officially as they had entered.

After Jaime had closed the door and heard the car leave, she broke down. She began to cry and shake, visibly affected by the surprise visit and prolonged interview. She gathered what was left of her composure and dialed Michael. He picked up on the first ring and she spoke.

"Michael, they were here and they think I shot that guy in Philly. I know they do, I'm sure, I'm so…"

Michael interrupted her, knowing he needed to calm her down.

"Who was there?" he answered in an anxious and concerned manner.

After a short hesitation, catching her breath, she replied.

"It was a guy named Treble and a guy who bore a very strong resemblance to you, so I assume it was your brother, Stephen."

"And what did they ask you?"

"They asked about the same things you and Kelly did, but they were very intense. They also asked about my guns, whereabouts and some other shit. Michael, I am very worried and scared."

He could tell that they had gotten to her; they had shaken her up and he was very concerned about not only her state of mind and well-being but also her guilt, if any. He questioned himself whether he was in denial about her involvement and also about his feelings toward her. As Chicago said in their top forty hit, he was "feeling stronger every day."

After the call, Michael thought long and hard about calling his brother, but he knew the stubbornness and dedication to his job would probably produce few, if any, answers. His relationship with Jaime had superseded the one with his brother, at least for the time being. This bothered him and he was now unsure of everything: his relationship with Jaime, her guilt or innocence, and even his decision to leave his job with the force. He had a lot of more thinking to do.

****

Later that afternoon, the four interviewers met back at the Roundhouse to compare notes. They went through specific questions, answers and impressions. When all was said and done, they were in total agreement about one fact. They all agreed that Jaime was probably the shooter at the Constitution Center and that she was also probably involved in the New Jersey slaying of Kim Carole.

Treble began after reading the notes.

"First, I would like to say that you two did a great job with your notes and observations," he said smiling at Stone and Kelly. "The fact that she appeared uptight, contradicted her earlier versions of her story, and couldn't remember how she paid for her groceries are all indications she is nervous. She knows we are on to her which will cause her to act more irrationally. It's my bet that she called Michael and that he will call us. When he does, I think Kelly should talk to him and tell him that her story checks out, to put her at ease. What do you three think?"

Davis, still upset at his brother and their drifting further apart, agreed, but he also voiced concern that they shouldn't use Michael to influence her behavior.

"He will probably advise her to get an attorney and not talk to us without him or her. He may even go so far as to advise her as to what we might do or not do, so we must wait until our warrant is signed before we bring her in. I would prefer if he is kept in the dark about that," still showing some of his protectiveness over his younger sibling.

The squad and some extras began checking phone records and credit cards and going over the interviews. The room was filled with the noise of shuffling papers, the tapping of keyboards and an occasional self-gratifying "yes." Davis and one of the lawyers were working on the search and seizure warrant, filling it out as information from the investigating team was handed to them. Dinner was ordered in, consumed and the work continued fervently. Slightly after ten o clock, the document was almost complete. An overhead projector displayed it on the wall for all to see the progress, giving them that extra feeling of accomplishment. Geek got up to stretch and walked to the back of the room. He eyed the document with pride.

United States District Court
City of Philadelphia
Case#534-7V1

In the matter of the search of:
Residence of Jaime Valle, suspect
Residence and property of Franklin Clayton, brother of Jaime Valle
Residence and property of Andrew and William Clayton, brothers of Jaime Valle
Residence and property of Robert Clayton, brother of Jaime Valle
Date and Time to be executed:
Copy of warrant and inventory left with:
Inventory made in the presence of:

Inventory of property taken and name of person(s) seized:
Date:
Executing Officer:

The list of items to be searched for had grown substantially. They were numerous.

1. Any firearms used for long distance purposes
2. Any ammunition used for the above firearms
3. Any receipts for firearms purchased or sold
4. Any storage containers hidden from plain sight
5. Any computers and hard drives
6. Any correspondence to and from said insurance companies
7. Any journals or day timers
8. Search of all vehicles owned or rented by any above mentioned persons
9. All credit card receipts held by Jaime Valle

The information and request for the warrant that would be presented to the judge was also in order. It mentioned that Jaime had been near or at the crime scene the day of the murder. She was an award winning marks person. She had purchased and owned a similar weapon. She had motive as her husband had died due to an insurance decision. She had ample opportunity to carry out the crime and no alibi as to her whereabouts at the time of the shootings. It was classic means, motive and opportunity, as well as a great deal of circumstantial evidence. The case was going cold and all involved were confident that they had the right suspect. The warrant would be served simultaneously to all the above named the following morning. With the packet of papers in his briefcase, Stephen went out into the late night darkness to disturb his favorite judge.

CHAPTER THIRTY-ONE

The next morning the teams who would serve the warrants gathered at the Roundhouse slightly after dawn. A mango colored sun squeezed its way through the skyscrapers of downtown Philadelphia, indicating it would be a damn nice day. Assignments were handed out. Four squads would visit each location, each squad consisting of an OCTF member, two Swat members and an assistant D.A. No trouble was expected, although an extra plainclothes officer accompanied the group to the twins' residence, that of Andrew and William. Geek made a note to his team that it was interesting that all four brothers had the first names of former presidents. All carried scrambled communication devices so as not to tip anyone off, just in case. Davis was concerned about his brother's whereabouts and had a car stationed at his residence. He would be closely watched.

The teams were scheduled to arrive simultaneously at 7:15 to prevent the targets from communicating or warning the others. Treble was with Davis and they were on the way to Jaime's house. If any evidence linking her to the crime was discovered, they would bring her downtown and put her ass in jail.

Zero hour arrived and there was knocking and announcements at each residence, with demands to gain entrance, search warrants in the hands of each agent. It was a well-coordinated search, the transmitters crackling with confirmations of safe entries. The Geek was manning the control center at the Roundhouse, watching videos as each SWAT officer was equipped with cameras on their helmets. It appeared to be going smoothly. Each of the residents was escorted outside as said items on the warrant were gathered and carried out to waiting vans that had arrived on scene moments after the first teams arrived.

Andrew and William lived down in South Jersey on a gentleman's farm. They grew produce during the season, boarded local horses and did the butchering for local deer hunters. Their property was the largest to search as it contained a main house, stables and a large shed.

Jaime was livid and was demanding to speak to her lawyer, but Davis said that after the search, she was free to do as she pleased. However, if anything was found to implicate her in the murder, her ass was his.

The searches were going as planned and, luckily, the media was still nowhere to be found. Davis prided himself in the professionalism, dedication and tight lipped protocol he had instilled in his team. They were living up to his expectations today. For the next several hours, the teams gathered and tagged all of the items that were listed in the warrant. They had computers, notes and receipts but, so far, no weapons or items to directly link any of them to the crime or the suspected cover up.

And then came a huge break. While the guys were searching the barn and stable area of the brothers, a homemade wooden cabinet was discovered in the back of a stall, under the watering trough. One of the searchers pulled a hammer and began smashing at the lock with extreme force. It opened.

Davis was outside glaring at Jaime when an excited voice blared through his hand held. He stepped away and lowered the volume as a feeling of energy ran through him. It was Kelly.

"Yo boss, we struck gold." His voice was loud and he was talking at Mach One speed. He continued.

"We found and opened a box, covered under the number four search item from the warrant. It has a rifle of the same caliber, ammo of the same caliber and a scope."

Before Kelly could utter another word, Davis spoke loudly into the speaker.

"Get it downtown pronto, and, Kelly, great fuckin' find."

Davis turned and approached Jaime, a sly smile on his face. He walked over, making a show of removing the handcuffs that were clipped on his belt.

"Miss Jaime Valle, please turn around. You are under arrest…"

His words dug deep into her like a switchblade penetrating soft flesh. She shook her head vehemently, starting to sob and deny his accusations. He nodded for an officer to assist him as she began to collapse. She was half-led and half-carried away in handcuffs and she was transported to the station. The gun and ammo would take priorities in the lab and the results would be forthcoming within an hour or two.

The search continued even though it appeared that the item they were wanting was now in their possession; Davis's gut told him that this was the weapon. Treble, who had been silent during the event, now approached Davis. Nothing needed to be added as they were both on the same page.

****

That same day, Marco Bracci was making his weekly trip to visit his father as he had sworn to do during his recent incarceration. During the long drive from New York, he worried about not living up to his father's expectations. It had been several months since the trial. Gando was still alive and one man had died due to a case of mistaken identity. The only thing he had done right was to hire some Asians for the hit in order to throw off any suspicions that it was a prototypical mob hit.

Upon his arrival, he knew the drill. He signed in at the visitor's area, went through the metal detectors and held his arms out as a scanner was passed along his clothing. He was ushered into the barren room sparsely decorated with only chairs, partitioned glass barriers and more chairs. Moments later, his father was brought to the seat opposite his, a large glass panel separating them. They both picked up the telephone receivers on their respective sides of the glass.

His father had only been there several months but looked like his age was beginning to creep up. He had been used to a free and flashy life style and his confinement was becoming evident. He regained his composure and smiled.

"Hey, dad, I put another five hundred into your account. Did they tell you?"

"Thanks, Marco. This freakin place is taking some time to get used to, but I'm doing okay. Had any luck with that old friend from the neighborhood that you're trying to find?"

"Nah, not yet, but I am confident I will find him. I put the word out but we'll hook up soon. I feel it."

"Good, good."

They went on to talk in a pre-arranged roundabout way about the business, the crews and how Marco was making out in regard to his new position. He knew his son still had a lot to learn and feared that one of his overzealous captains might want to take over the family business. Marco had been prepared for this. His father was still respected and making everyone money even though he was not around. As long as that continued, things would be fine. Rumor had it that the elder Bracci had enlisted the aid of an anonymous group of hit men who would make sure that everything remained in place. Regardless if it was rumor or fact, so far nothing had changed in the hierarchy of his organization.

They talked some sports and about the status of the appeal which his lawyer was diligently working on. Before leaving, he swore that he would find his friend sooner rather than later and their reunion might even be fun! He said goodbye and headed toward the exit and the long drive back to New York.

CHAPTER THIRTY-TWO

The news of the arrest was no longer contained and the news trucks and media clogged the steps of the Roundhouse. A press conference was set for the afternoon. They needed to wait for the ballistics reports to see what additional charges might be filed against Jaime. The New Jersey State police had been filled in on the day's events. They too were hoping that they could match the bullet that had killed Kim Carole.

Davis was over-enthusiastic and anxious about the forensic testing. He followed the two technicians around as they test fired the bullets found with the rifle into the tank of water at the back of the room. They then retrieved them to put under the stereo microscope to compare them side by side. After they both examined them and turned the eyepiece, there was no doubt. The bullets were a match. Davis fired a fist into the air and almost ran toward the elevator to spread the news.

He arrived upstairs and waved for the awaiting group to convene in the usual place, Conference Room B. They anxiously followed and waited for the results. But his shitfaced grin already told the story.

"I would first like to thank all of you for the dedication and hard work that led to this discovery. The bullet matches the one found in our insurance casualty and we are waiting for the results from Kim Carole. As we speak, we are checking for prints and DNA from the weapon and scope, and we are going through receipts found to match the purchase of any of the ammunition. I have called a press conference for the five o clock news and would like you all there. It was a team effort and I want the public to acknowledge that fact."

A small round of applause, fist bumping and high fives spread around the room. The desk phone rang, silencing the crowd and momentarily breaking the celebratory mood. The Geek answered and picked up the receiver. He called Davis over and whispered in his ear. His mood changed suddenly and he left the room at a frenzied pace.

Wheeling toward him was his brother, Michael. Looks to kill adorned his face. He had seen this look before.

"What the hell is going on, bro," Michael stated in a demeaning and demanding tone.

"My office, right now," he fired back with just as much urgency.

When Michael pulled up to the desk and Stephen took his seat, they began.

"Shut the hell up, slow down and listen." Stephen said in the familiar tone that his brother recognized. It was how he began when a lecture was forthcoming. He continued.

"First of all, I would like to mention that I have stayed out of your little fling with our main suspect. Give me that. Secondly, the evidence that we gathered today looks pretty freakin bad. We have a weapon, ammunition and are in the process of matching her prints. Denial is a bad thing, Michael. I stayed out of your business, watched you make some bad decisions in regards to your career with the team, and get romantically involved when it's now obvious you shouldn't have."

Michael held back, waiting his brother's lecture out till he was done.

"She is a killer. Of not one but of two people and those I have arrested in the past do not make these actions spontaneously. They are well thought out and there is always, I mean always, a strong motive. You have no idea how it hurt me when you made your mind up, but because I respect you and what you have accomplished, I let things be. Not only am I proud of you but I love you."

Michael gathered his thoughts as well as his hostilities and responded.

"I get it. But you had always been the good and favorite child. You were smart. You always dated the hot babes. You played baseball and football and were damn good at both. Tell me…how could I live up to that?" Michael stared at his brother's intense face and continued.

"So I tried to do my best, but it was just never as good as yours. I wasn't as popular, wasn't as athletically talented and didn't date nearly as

The group gathered around the podium used for such conferences, embossed with the seal of the Philadelphia Police Department. Treble turned to Stone and whispered, "I guess this is why they call this city Killadelphia." She wasn't amused

On cue, Commissioner Sullivan, decked out in his dress blues for the national TV audience, approached the microphone. Throngs of microphones were held up like lighters at a Springsteen concert, each displaying the name of the respective stations. He proudly began.

"Good afternoon to all and we are pleased to inform you that we have some breaking news in regard to a case that has captured the nation's attention. Earlier this afternoon a suspect was apprehended without incident in regard to the shooting that happened at the Constitution Center here in our great city of Philadelphia."

Flashbulbs lighted the late afternoon sky and questions began to fill the quiet venue. Sullivan held out his open hands in a gesture made to quiet the crowd before he continued. They complied and he continued.

"Standing behind me is part of the team that made this arrest possible and I would like you to hear the details from those who were directly responsible for solving this heinous crime."

He went on to introduce the group behind him as they stood stoically, keeping on their best professional faces. When he was done, he beckoned Davis to replace him at the podium and fill the press in on more of the details they craved. He was popular and well-respected with the local media, having solved two major cases in the past two years. Flashbulbs rekindled as Davis readied to address the crowd of media hounds and news junkies.

"This morning, a number of warrants were served to various individuals who we believed had critical information and evidence regarding the case of the Constitution Center shootings that occurred last fall. With help from the FBI and various law enforcement agencies, all cooperating with a common goal, we are delighted to announce that an arrest has been made in the case."

Before he could utter another word, questions erupted from the crowd. Davis lowered his head and stepped back from the podium, a sign that he would not continue until the noise level subsided. It did in an instant. He stepped back and faced the crowd and resumed speaking.

"I would like to ask that all questions be held until the completion of this statement." He then proceeded where he had left off.

"Our suspect is Miss Jaime Valle, a resident of Camden County, New Jersey." He avoided her address to slow the throng of news trucks and reporters from swarming her location.

"She is widowed and has no children. The personal tragedy of losing her husband was a trigger that set her off and she felt it necessary to take revenge on those she believed were the cause of this tragedy. We have in our possession the weapon that we believe was used along with other evidence we cannot disclose at this time. We also believe that she acted alone and is also a suspect in another homicide which we and the New Jersey State Police are collaborating upon. The charges will be murder in the first degree, lying in wait and other charges of weapon violations may also be attached."

Just then a tall, well-dressed and slightly tanned man made his way through the crowd. His passage was cleared by news reporters who more closely resembled a mass of zombies following their leader to a boiling cauldron of human flesh.

"It's Manning, T. Hudson Manning," and attention was refocused to the all-star attorney who now captivated the crowd.

Manning was quite an anomaly. Like his unrelated namesakes who could lead a fourth quarter comeback with almost certain regularity, he could sway a jury in less time than it took the state of Florida to tally up election ballots during a presidential election. And although he dressed in Brooks Brother's garb, he was an attorney "for the people." He represented the underdog rather than guilty upper crust high-profile criminals who tended to buy justice.

His record was almost perfect. The only case he had lost in the past decade occurred in the state of Pennsylvania, which was the speculation

CHAPTER THIRTY-THREE

"What a fucked up day," Davis conveyed to Stone as they deftly picked up the noodles from the Pad Thai they were sharing.

"What's up with that asshole lawyer?" she asked as she stared into his eyes.

"He loves the spotlight and, unfortunately, he is a damned good attorney," Davis replied as he slightly shook his head.

Stone understood all of his moods and idiosyncrasies. She knew he needed not to over think or project what might happen during the trial in the coming months. He had done his job, as had the team, in the investigation and arrest process that had taken them to this point. It wasn't that he needed reassurance; he knew that he had done everything possible to provide the evidence necessary to make the strong case. She placed her hand over his with an encouraging squeeze that made him smile and derail his train of thought.

"Thanks, Ash. You know all my buttons. I don't know if that's good or bad," he said in a favorable fashion. She loved when he complimented her as he so was tough to please. They finished up, paid the bill and made a quick detour to grab some Ben and Jerry's for dessert.

They arrived back at his place, kicked off their shoes and couched out. With no desire to watch any news, they opted for some mindless reality show, but never made it past the first few seconds. After two spoons of ice cream, the third dripped down Ashley's chin but Davis chivalrously prevented it from reaching her neck, his warm lips melting it as his tongue cleaned every drop. That was about all it took. Who cared if it melted?

They disrobed as if it was an Olympic event and as if time was of the essence. Their bodies were tightly pressed against each other as their lips randomly met and parted in a teasing manner. Davis worked his way down from her neck, to her breasts and then to the center of her sensuality, met by not one ounce of resistance. Her movements coincided with his actions, knowing her body like it was his own. She pulled his head into her, asking him to stop at the same time. (Do women *ever know what they want?*) She climaxed quickly, her body and breathing slowing down to a standstill. She quivered and then fell silent, taking in the pleasure and passion.

She regained her strength, or at least what was left of it, and returned the favor. For spite and the fact that she hated waste, she took a mouthful of still cold ice cream and surrounded his obvious excitement. He was surprised, chilled, and startled, but remained erect. After her playfulness, he returned back to his normal state. They kissed and teased for a bit longer before retiring to bed. The passion had yet to subside.

Just as his head hit the pillow, the cell phone rang. Ashley rolled over away from him. He almost always picked up, especially if it was work related. He glanced at the screen and waited for the caller to speak.

"Yo, bro, really hope I am not disturbing anything," came the familiar voice of his brother. "Got a minute for me?" he said in such a way that refusal was not an option.

"I fucked up, I know and I realize you saw it coming. I'm different from you and obviously a lot needier. I'll forgo the psychobabble."

Stephen jumped in, cutting off the upcoming sentence.

"Blood is thicker and all that crap, Michael. I do not need nor ask for any reason for what you did. It was something that I thought, or at least hoped, would work itself out. Now it has. As far as I am concerned, the whole thing is in the past." His sincerity in that statement was obvious. Throughout all that had happened, the love for his brother never wavered, although he did question his assessment of the situation.

"Thanks, bro," was all that he said, knowing that it was all that needed to be said. He added that if he needed any help in the future of the investigation, he should just ask. Ashley listened but remained silent. Nothing needed to be said on her part, either.

****

Treble and Dubbin didn't have nearly as much fun. Sarah was slightly annoyed at the arrogance and attitude he expressed after Manning rained on their parade. She thought it unnecessary to, as she put it, fuel the fire and cause a scene. Especially for the media who tends to side with the underdog. They hadn't been dating nearly as long as Stone and Davis and, as many relationships begin, sex was a big part of it. But Sarah and Treble had quite different personalities. Who said opposites attract?

She was sensitive, thoughtful and modest. He was more cocky, a bit insensitive and a true alpha male. He was polite, opened doors and treated her like the classy woman she was. He respected both her work as well as her intelligence and common sense. But she hated arrogance and cockiness, which is exactly what Treble had exhibited earlier today. Rather than playing the "headache card," she used the "it's that time of the month" card, which actually is the best one in the deck. PMS is one of man's biggest fears.

So he took the offered rain check and decided to go it alone and grab a burger and beer. Maybe he would get lucky, he thought.

****

Unlike Philadelphia, it seemed like spring and summer were the only seasons in Florida. Void of down jackets and ear muffs, the girls were working hard during the day and playing even harder at night. The duo of Abby and Bryant had now become a trio, having bonded well with Allie, even in spite of the fact that most men had no clue that this phenomenon even existed. Ever hear of a "woman cave?" I didn't think so.

The trio fashioned themselves as a smaller version of *Sex in the City* but in reality it was *Sex in the 'Burbs*. None of the three really cared for anything long term, as their business came first and foremost. As time went on, they shared more and more with each other about their past lives. And, most importantly, they were making money. South Florida was recovering from the housing and job recession of the recent past and there is never a shortage of single women looking for a guy with money. Who cares about politically correct things to say these days, anyway?

Two mornings a week, the trio met at a French patisserie for coffee, croissants and fresh pastries. It took five days a week at the gym to make all of those fresh pastries disappear from destination hips, but it was worth it.

That morning they began to reminisce about Philadelphia, which had almost disappeared from their memory cells, especially the past two years. Allie only knew bits and pieces of the Gando story, but she really didn't ask many questions. If Bryant had wanted her to know more she would have told her. As Yogi Berra once said, "we made too many wrong mistakes."

"Ya know, I still check the Philly papers on the Internet once in a while and still haven't heard about Julian or the guys he put away. I seriously doubt that all was forgotten," Bryant said in a philosophical yet matter of fact way.

"Believe me; we will hear about it if anything happens, seeing it was national news last year. But it's funny, too. It almost seems like another lifetime," Abby commented, her observation spot-on.

The trio talked about where to go for happy hour that evening, as hump day was always a good night out. They decided to meet after work, paid the check and headed off to the strip mall to begin the day.

* *

Several towns away, Gando and Crello were having breakfast before their day at the restaurant began. They had found the only spot that had passable bagels, something sorely missed south of Brooklyn, New York.

CHAPTER THIRTY-FOUR

It seemed to become a yearly tradition of having high profile homicide cases on the court dockets in the City of Brotherly Love. Even the city's nickname was becoming a misnomer, as love didn't seem so apt anymore.

As the summer hit full stride, the trial of the year was getting ready to begin. Coverage was insane by the national media. People Magazine, the National Enquirer, True TV, and the Philadelphia press had all jumped on the bandwagon. They ran interviews with Jaime's friends, delved into her past and even Dr. Phil broke down her psychological profile. Her lawyer, T. Hudson Manning, helped fuel the fire, portraying her as a woman destroyed by the system that she trusted without question.

Surprisingly, she had been granted bail, partially because of the fact that Manning had presented a stellar argument for her and partially because the OCTF felt she was not a flight risk. Also, the team might be able to gather more insight and evidence to use at the trial. Michael was now back with the team part time and working with them, so they believed that allowing bail was a good risk.

Another factor was that the New Jersey authorities were foaming at the mouth, as they had second dibs on bringing Jaime to trial. The evidence in the killing of Kim Carole also coincided with the homicide across the river, although placing her at the scene was impossible to prove. Still, if she was not convicted in Philadelphia, which they believed to be the proverbial slam dunk, they would try her in Camden County on charges of murder.

Jaime learned to play the part of the woman who had her life turned upside down by an evil and greedy corporation that had put profit margin ahead of human life. We all root for the underdog. Her story spread throughout the country, and, although the authorities painted her as a cold blooded killer, the working class public spoke in her favor. "Man on the street" interviews gave her credit for standing up against "big brother" or against the giant corporations that take advantage of the "little guy." Her cardigan sweater and newly added eyewear gave her a look of naïve innocence. She was good at her new role and Manning could sell ice to an Eskimo.

Meanwhile, Gerry Brett, the Federal prosecutor, was well aware of the image he would be up against. He was confident with his case, but was wary and challenged by his adversary. Emotions often trump facts and that is what he was up against. However, he and his assistants understood this and would prepare their case accordingly. He was also pretty damn good and competitive as well.

Jaime was standoffish in regard to Michael, having doubts if she could trust him. He had never abandoned her during this whole ordeal, which elicited conflicting emotions about his loyalties. Michael was able to bring out her emotions, honesty and true feelings and she worried about the consequences. Rightly so, and so did Manning. He was concerned but said if, stressing the word *if,* and when she might see him that she must avoid any talk about the impending case. That was easier said than done.

In what seemed like no time, the day of the trial arrived and the national media swarmed into Philadelphia like a plague of locusts upon the Egyptians. The city leaders were happy in the sense that it would add to the sagging economy, but if the outcome was less than expected, they would slip several notches down on the list of safest places to live.

✳✳✳✳✳✳✳✳✳✳✳✳✳✳✳✳✳✳✳✳✳✳✳✳

The presiding judge, Roderick Harris, was fair and impartial, maybe too much so, according to some. He tapped the gavel and brought the courtroom to order. Sitting to his left was Manning and his team, not quite what O.J.'s dream team was, but more than sufficient. Again, you drink. They toasted to their friendship and bonding, pounding down shots of Patron as if they were on a Mexican hayride.

Before the ladies passed out or made total fools of themselves, the bartender called a cab and had two of the Chippendale-like bouncers safely place them in the back seat. Before hitting the pillow, Bern gave herself one more gold star for the job well done, and the best part is that no one knew a rat's ass of how she spent part of her summer vacation.

on the cheek. Gando spoke in a low woozy voice as the anesthetic began to lose its hold.

"That bitch who shot me was Pudello's daughter."

"Freakin A" was the most fitting response that Jake could muster.

"And unless someone had recognized me and told her, it was just dumb luck," Gando said in a speculative way. Continuing, he said that he would tell Pacone he was supposed to meet a woman there but two Latin-looking guys showed up, shot me, and stole the car. When I get out of here, the bitch is mine."

Jake remained several minutes longer in order to mention two things. The first was they had their most successful night of sales ever, which did bring a small bit of satisfaction to Gando. The second was that he would make some calls and see if she was still local and put word out to all of his cronies to do whatever it takes to find her.

Pacone entered and thumbed Jake that it was his turn. He left and headed out of the hospital to make those calls. As promised, Gando gave Pacone the story about the carjacking, watching as he took dubious notes and questioned him about every detail. Gando had not lost his knack for deception and he knew that Pacone bought the whole cock and bull story. Before leaving, he told Gando that he would be on it and an arrest would be his top priority. Gando then fell back to sleep, his thoughts centered on the torturous revenge he would plan for B, or who he now remembered as Bernadette Madison.

******

The next morning, Allie noticed she was out of coffee and told Bern she would get some and be right back. Bern asked her to grab a newspaper, which was kind of odd as she really didn't follow the news. Feeling she needed to make the request sound more credible, she added that she wanted the real estate section to see what was available, just in case. Allie gave it no more thought, exited the condo toward the car and drove to the market.

When Allie returned, Bern had showered and dressed. Allie threw some assorted breakfast items and the paper down on the counter, taking the coffee pods with her to brew several cups. Bern pulled the paper out from under the pile, her hands shaking a bit unsteadily, not knowing what, if any, story she might find. Buried in the local news section, a small byline read "Local Man Found Shot near Desolate Construction Site." Reading further, the only thing she learned was that he alive and in critical condition and that no identification was found on the body. It concluded saying that police suspect a carjacking as the motive and the vehicle, an Audi A5, had yet to be found. The story concluded with a local number to call if the car was spotted. She felt her heart rate accelerate and she hadn't even had her morning blast of coffee.

CHAPTER FORTY-THREE

Two weeks post-verdict, the jury would have its final responsibility, that of imposing a sentence on Jaime. Unlike the long trial proceedings, this phase turned out to last shortly under two days, including the victim impact statement, psychiatrists' recommendations and the scornful rhetoric of a beaten prosecutor who was seeking the maximum ten year sentence in a medium-to-high level facility.

The jurors sat patiently listening, several taking notes, and were dismissed for lunch, which they would have brought to them as they deliberated. The OCTF was again absent, having been called to work on the homicide of a federal undercover agent who had infiltrated a terrorist cell and was then exposed. Treble attended, offering testimony and the suggestion that she be incarcerated for the maximum sentence asked for by the prosecution. He had testified that he believed "this crime was well planned, well executed and every attempt had been made to hide evidence." His statement was written into the record of proceedings.

When the jurors returned from their home away from home, they again handed a slip of paper to the bailiff, this one containing their sentencing recommendations. Although Judge Harris had the right to toss out their suggestion and impose his own, he had never done so during his history on the bench. He was a Constitutionalist, believing strongly in the phrasing that said it was a government by the people and for the people. And he lived by his words. The defendant was asked to stand and Judge Harris read the sentence.

"It has been determined by a jury of your peers that you be committed to an institution for treatment for a period of no less than two and no more than three years, or until you are deemed fit to rejoin society with the pronouncement that you will present no harm to others." His gavel

261

came down swiftly and authoritatively, ending the trial of the year. He vanished into his chambers before the anticipated outbreak of bedlam became too loud.

News made it back to the media in light speed. Across the Delaware River in Trenton, the ruling had a disappointing reality. The New Jersey state troopers would not be able to indict her at the current time because by doing so they would be chastised for attacking a woman who was institutionalized. On a positive note, when Jaime's sentence expired, there would be no statute of limitation regarding to the murder of Kim Carole. They would have at least two years to build a case and they planned to do just that.

****

Davis and Stone sat at one of their favorite lunch spots. He was having a chicken salad on rye toast, and she a blackened chicken salad. She stole one of his French fries smothered in ketchup and then spoke.

"Let's skip the talk about the trial. Why don't we just take one of those sun- and sex-filled long weekends? I don't care where we go, let's just get out of town."

Davis mimicked her by grabbing a fry with an even larger helping of ketchup, wiped the drippings off his chin and responded to her comment after looking at the time on his cell phone.

"Either finish up quick or take it with you. We can be at the travel agency before our lunch break is done."

Smiling, she grabbed him by the collar, kissed him, picked up the check and they were on their way.

18902833R00142

Made in the USA
Charleston, SC
26 April 2013